Only a Bridesmaid

Only a Bridesmaid

by

Haley Donnell

2024

ONLY A BRIDESMAID

ISBN 13: 978-1-63679-642-0

This Trade Paperback Original Is Published By
Bold Strokes Books, Inc.
P.O. Box 249
Valley Falls, NY 12185

First Edition: May 2024

Credits
Production Design: Stacia Seaman
Cover Design by Tammy Seidick

Acknowledgments

I would like to thank my parents and my partner for sticking with me when I had my nose in a book or couldn't get a story idea out of my head.

I'd also like to give a big thank you to the BSB team, especially Sandy, for taking a chance on me and making my dream of being a published author come true.

Finally, thank you to you, the reader, for being part of this story with me.

To my mom, for always believing in me.

CHAPTER ONE

This is weird.

Like, super weird.

Like, weird to the point that I keep glancing at the door to make sure I still have an exit route.

Part of it is Eric himself, for sure. He is the most average guy I have ever seen, like he was cut out of a magazine. His blond hair is perfectly in place, probably courtesy of about a pound of gel, and his teeth are so straight I wouldn't be surprised if he confessed to having had them all removed and replaced with realistic porcelain veneers.

The weirdest part, though, is the job he is offering me.

"It's just for a week," he explains. "Plus two meetings before we go to the island. One group meeting, then a party to make it realistic." He smiles, showing off those creepy teeth. His whole demeanor is confident and self-satisfied, as if to say how great a fiancé he is to be doing this.

"I'm sorry." My words are insincere as I push my chair away from the table and reach for my empty cup. Our meeting is in a crowded café in Portland's Hawthorne District, and the fact that we're surrounded by people is the only reason I didn't walk out the second I saw Eric's creepy smile. "But I think I'll pass."

"I'll pay ten thousand dollars," Eric continues calmly. I

sink back into my seat and meet his too-blue eyes. Ten thousand dollars is a lot of money. I work as a super-small-time actor and drama teacher and live frugally. Ten thousand dollars can pay at least three months of my bills.

I just hope I don't have to sell my soul.

"I'm listening." I half-sigh. "Can you start from the beginning?"

"Of course." His smile is syrupy and clearly shows he finds my inability to remember what he said just a few minutes ago to be a very problematic quality. But hey, it isn't my fault that I had to spend my time wondering about his dentistry instead of listening to him. "So, Hannah and I are getting married in a month, and she doesn't have anyone who can be her bridesmaids." He pauses to arrange his face into what he probably assumes is a sympathetic expression and I nod.

I wonder, though, what kind of woman would not only agree to marry this creep, but also wouldn't have friends or relatives to be her bridesmaids. *Is she also a straight-toothed pompous weirdo?* Probably.

"I want her to have the full wedding experience," Eric continues. "Bachelorette party—although it should be low-key—pictures, speeches, all that. I don't want anyone to look back on our wedding photos and wonder about Hannah, you know?" He gives another disturbing smile.

"How…*sweet* of you."

He doesn't seem to notice I'm being insincere because he nods. His motivations are questionable, though. He seems more interested in appearances than in ensuring his fiancée actually enjoys the wedding. He reminds me of a director I had early in my career who was more interested in appearing *artsy* and *deep* than in putting on a good performance.

"Anyway, ten grand for a week of work is a pretty good deal, wouldn't you say?"

"It's very generous." I'm still on the fence, though. Hannah and Eric's wedding is supposed to take place on a private island in the Caribbean, which seems like a prime location for my murder if the future Mrs. Creep is as weird as this guy. I can see the headlines already.

"Great!" Eric claps his hands. "*Perfect*. Oh, and I almost forgot, I have a picture of Hannah somewhere in here." He digs through his wallet and hands me a passport-sized photograph.

The woman in the photo is beautiful. Truly. Like Eric, she's blond and blue-eyed, but unlike Eric, she looks more like a Disney princess than a villain in a James Bond movie. She's posing for the picture; she sits on a block in front of a forest scene. What I notice most about her, though, is that behind her smile and folded hands, there's a spark in her eyes. She looks like she's thinking of a hilarious private joke.

Something else about her wakes my protective instincts. I don't know her story or why she's marrying Eric, but I think she needs some help. *Maybe she hasn't noticed how weird her fiancé is.* And just like that, I'm too curious to turn this job down.

"I'm looking forward to working with you." I return the picture and pause to consider my next words. "I was also wondering if you have all the other bridesmaids sorted out. I have someone I could recommend."

"I still have an open spot and time is running a little low. Do you have a picture of your recommendation?"

"Sure." I find my phone and a picture of me and my best friend, Jen. In the photo, we're smiling with our arms around each other in front of Multnomah Falls.

"A Chinese girl…" Eric takes my phone and zooms in on Jen's face. "Perfect."

I have sudden urge to punch Eric in his perfect teeth. *Diversity* must be the reason he's hiring me, too. I'm half-French, half-Indian and have the kind of features that guys like Eric call *exotic*, although not to my face.

I know he's rich. When we first introduced ourselves, Eric said his family owns a chain of hotels. Maybe this is his attempt to not look racist in front of a bunch of investors. I am even less excited to be involved, or to drag Jen into this, if that's the reason he's hiring me.

But I suppose I am using him, too, for his money.

"Hmm," I say, instead of any of that. I don't like not speaking my mind, but I also don't want to get off on the wrong foot with my new employer moments after agreeing to take this job. Plus, I doubt I could change his mind.

"Tell your friend she's hired." Eric swipes to the next picture without asking permission. "I'll need to have a phone call with her to confirm some details, but it should be fine."

"Great." I flash a disingenuous smile and snatch my phone from his hand before he can look at any more of my private pictures. I shove the phone into my pocket. Jen is *absolutely* going to kill me for getting her involved in this nonsense, but I need my friend by my side. *Plus, a paid week on an island can't be all bad.* We just need to avoid the groom.

Eric gets to his feet, already ready to leave. "I have to ask." I tilt my head to the side. "How does Hannah feel about this? Didn't she want to interview her own bridesmaids?"

"Hannah is embarrassed. I'm sure you can understand why. So, I told her I would just take care of this for her." He pauses. I get the feeling he's waiting for me to praise him for being an excellent fiancé. I don't say a word, though, and he pushes on. "Anyway, she's a nice girl. Just socially awkward."

What a nice thing to say about one's future spouse. I make another noncommittal noise, soldier through a handshake, and allow Eric to escort me to the door, which he opens for me with a flourish and a wide grin. He seems like the kind of guy who shows his support of women through misplaced chivalry instead of actual respect. I could be wrong, though. We did just meet.

"I'll expect to see you at the introductory session on the nineteenth. I'll send you all the details via email."

"Okay."

"Well, thank you again, Milly."

"It's Meli." Although my full name is Amelie, I prefer the short, quirky nickname in my day-to-day life. At least when people bother to pronounce it correctly.

"Sure. Have a nice day, Milly." With that, he ushers me out the door.

I'm annoyed. I glance at his retreating frame, then hug my raincoat close and walk in the opposite direction. It's March, which is a particularly miserable month in Portland. It's drizzling sleet, which falls in loud drops on my hood. As I walk toward the bus station, I dig my phone out of my pocket and take a deep breath. I need to be calm if I'm going to explain all this to Jen.

"'Sup?" Jen sounds a little distracted. *Oh.* Unlike me with my flexible schedule of drama classes and occasional late nights when I'm working on a play, Jen has a regular nine-to-five job as a web designer, and it's the middle of the day. In my haste, I forgot she's working now.

"How would you like to spend a weekend on a tropical island and get paid ten thousand dollars for it?" I use my best sales associate tone of voice. If Jen refuses to do this, which would be understandable, it'd be worse than showing up for dress rehearsal without knowing my lines. Maybe it's time for a *Buddy-Up.*

There's a pause on the other end and a bit of clacking. Then Jen comes more clearly on the line.

"Sorry, can you repeat that?"

"I just got offered the job of a lifetime. *And* I got *you* on board. We're playing the part of bridesmaids at a destination wedding in the Caribbean. It's a whole week next month, plus two meetings here in Portland."

"Like, bridesmaids in a movie? Extras or something?"

"Noooo." I bite my lip. "Bridesmaids at a real wedding, and for a real woman."

"Why doesn't she invite her own friends?" Jen sounds very suspicious. "Is she, like, some bridezilla who lost all her friends in the wedding planning process?"

I am suddenly defensive of Hannah. Whatever she is, she's probably *not* a bridezilla. She didn't even want to interview her own bridesmaids.

"No. It sounds like she really doesn't have friends, and her future husband decided to hire us. But she seems nice." *From her picture anyway.* "I'm sure there's a good reason why she doesn't have people to invite. And she's super gorgeous."

"Okay, I get it now!" A hint of a laugh creeps into Jen's voice. "We're doing this because you've fallen madly in love with an engaged woman, and you want me to wing-woman you at her wedding."

"No!" *Jen's uncomfortably close to the truth.* "I'm just trying to help my best friend with a little extra income and a cool vacation. Come on! It'll be fun!"

"You're selling this too hard." *Also true*. "What's the catch?"

"The groom is a bit of a jerk face," I admit. "Like Chaz."

I can practically hear Jen shudder over the phone. Chaz went to college with us here in Portland. We weren't friends with him by any means, but he somehow was still around a lot, making vaguely racist and sexist comments and telling us loudly about his *lit* weekend plans. He was never physically aggressive, but his behavior was disturbing enough that we reported him to campus security so he'd leave us alone. Ever since, we've used him as a yardstick to measure how problematic the people in our lives are, on a scale from zero to Chaz.

"But," I add quickly, "this is a *Buddy-Up* situation."

Jen sighs loudly, but she agrees. She has to. *Buddy-Ups* are something we invented back in college. When we were thrown together in the same dorm as nervous first-year students, we decided to have each other's backs, based primarily on the fact that we didn't know anyone else. So, when one of us really wanted to go to an interesting party or take a challenging class, that person declared a *Buddy-Up* and the other person had to say yes. The system has gotten us into a couple of scrapes over the years, but the tradition has been positive enough to continue.

Jen and I chat for a few more minutes, then say our good-byes when the bus arrives. I'm beyond interested in how this wedding will go. Some of my friends have gotten married, but they opted for small, casual affairs in parks or in the forest. The last time I attended a big shebang like this I was a flower girl, so it'll be fun to attend as a bridesmaid this time. And a Caribbean island certainly doesn't hurt.

Yet more than anything else, I'm intrigued by the idea of meeting Hannah. I have no reason to believe so, but I'm somehow sure she and I are going to get along.

Chapter Two

I'm not even being dramatic when I say that this is my literal nightmare.

Literally. I've had this nightmare.

Eric and I sit side by side on a couch in his favorite café, L'Amour. He thinks it's my favorite too, though not because of anything I've said. I have a death grip on one of his hands and he sips his coffee with the other.

"Are you sure this is the right thing to do?"

"Hannah, honey, of course, it is. You don't want to be the only bride with no bridesmaids, do you?"

"No." Although I'd rather not have a wedding at all. "But I still think, maybe a smaller wedding—"

"Honey." Eric sets down his coffee cup and squeezes my hand. "I'm so lucky to have such a down-to-earth fiancée. Most women in your place would be falling over themselves to outspend all their friends!" He sweeps his free hand in a wide circle as if to show all the spending of these fictional women. "But I know you wouldn't really be happy with a small ceremony."

I probably would be, but that's beside the point. Eric's the head of a huge chain of luxury hotels inherited from his father, and this wedding is a great publicity opportunity for my fiancé. *He* wouldn't be happy with a small wedding, so therefore, neither would I. If I don't go along with all this fanfare, I might spend the rest of my married life hearing about how I inconvenienced my husband from the very beginning with my nerves. Plus, my parents are looking forward to a big wedding.

"It's just—"

The door swings open. A young woman with red hair and green eyes enters. She waves to Eric and prances toward us. We have a full view of her very tight top, a skirt that could pass for a headband, and sky-high stilettos.

"Hi!" Her gaze is completely focused on Eric. If I were the jealous type, that would probably bother me. Maybe I should be bothered anyway.

"Hi." Eric beams at her. He has a very charming smile, and he knows it from all the times it has gotten him his own way. "Hannah, this is Crystal, one of your bridesmaids."

Crystal appraises me. She probably sees a small, shy woman who won't be too much of a threat to her. I want to say there's a little more to me than that, but I don't. I get the feeling she's pleased with what she finds, because she smiles insincerely and extends one small hand. "Nice to meet you!"

"Mm-hmm." I'm not being rude—not that I would mind being rude to this woman—but I often have trouble getting words out in front of people. This inability to speak my mind in social situations is a huge problem. Once I get to know someone, I'm more able to say what I'm thinking, but so much of life seems to involve talking to strangers—waiters, new coworkers, Eric's business associates, raving lunatics, and so on. My inability to speak confidently to strangers strains everything from my life at work to my personal relationships.

I never could put this shyness, or social anxiety, or general dislike of social situations, into words. Nor do I want to. It's as much a part of me as the color of my eyes or my love of Harry Potter—even if it is a part I don't love.

"Well." Crystal sits close to Eric. A little too close. "Are you staying?" She bats her long fake eyelashes at him.

"No." Eric sounds a little disappointed. *Huh.* "I want you all to get to know Hannah a little."

I'm saved from having to listen to any more of Crystal's attempts at flirtation by the arrival of two more women. The first woman is short and dark-haired, with a round face. She wears a pair of slacks with a fitted blouse, and inexplicably carries an umbrella. Most Portlanders don't carry them since the rain here is usually light, and I wonder why she chose to bring one. Maybe she doesn't mind standing out, a quality I find both impressive and a little scary. Personally, I ditched all my umbrellas when I arrived here a few years ago so that I would be more invisible. She catches sight of me and smiles kindly, then steps to the side to let another woman in out of the rain.

The friend wears a blue Ravenclaw scarf, which gives me a little hope. A fellow Harry Potter fan would definitely help me feel more comfortable in this incredibly strange situation. The scarf is paired with a long gray raincoat, which is fitted, and a pair of dark purple leggings.

She's also beautiful. She has long, dark hair that cascades from her hood like she's the star in a shampoo commercial. Her dark brown eyes are framed by long, very real eyelashes and her skin is a soft tan.

"Hi!" she says brightly as she walks over to us. "I'm Meli, and this is Jen." She extends her hand, fingers curled in, and it takes me a beat to realize she wants a fist bump, which I give her. Something about the interaction makes me smile. I don't meet a lot of adult women who give fist bumps, at least not in the world of Eric's business associates, but I like it.

"This is Hannah," Eric says, and I realize I didn't introduce myself. My cheeks warm as I reach for my hot chocolate. I wrap my hands around the mug so I'll have something to do with them. I want to contribute some witty comment, maybe a joke about how since Meli is a Ravenclaw, I would assume she could figure out my name herself. Instead, I just stare at my drink, blushing.

One more woman hurries in and shucks her raincoat at the door before joining us. She's a pretty woman with long braids on one side and close-shaved hair on the other. Eric introduces her as Charlie, but we have no time for conversation. Eric stands and smiles his charming smile around the circle.

"Thank you all for coming," he says. "Please, chat with Hannah a little and get to know her." He raises a hand to the side of his mouth as though sharing a secret. "She gets a bit tight-lipped when she's nervous, so just persevere. Remember, we want it to really seem like you all know each other. Make sure to take at least a few pictures! Okay. Ladies, enjoy yourselves."

He sees himself out. A strange part of me wishes he would stay, so I know someone, even as another part of me is glad to see the back of him. I wish he hadn't made me sound so awkward in front of these women, who are already strangers to me. *Oh no.*

"So, let's get something to drink?" Crystal breaks the silence. Three of the women stand eagerly, but for some reason Meli, the Ravenclaw, stays seated next to me.

"Jen, will you get me a mocha?"

Jen nods to Meli and follows the women walking away. I wish Meli would leave, too. She seems nice, but now I either have to think of something to say to her or sit here in awkward silence.

"I like your scarf!" I blurt. A momentary rush of pride floods me. I didn't second-guess myself and I managed to say something. What I said even makes sense in the context.

"Oh, this old thing?" Meli dramatically flips the end over her shoulder. "This is only my favorite piece of clothing. I mean,

JK is a bit problematic with some of the things she's said online, but since I already own it…Are you a fan?"

I nod emphatically. "*Mm-hmm.*"

"And are you a fellow Ravenclaw?"

"No." My voice is soft, but I *am* speaking. *Thank goodness.* "I'm, um, more of a Hufflepuff."

Meli leans back, sweeping her gaze over me. When Crystal looked me over, she sized me up as if I was a threat. Meli's gaze makes me feel…seen. Meli nods.

"You have that patient, hardworking look about you."

I smile. I'm glad Meli chose the positive traits of Hufflepuff, or what I find to be positive, instead of the reputation Hufflepuff seems to have for being boring or unimportant.

"Um, did you know that Tonks is…um, also a Hufflepuff?" I'm staring at my drink, but at least I'm still talking.

"I did not." Meli actually sounds interested. She shifts to face me, and I turn toward her a little more, too. "So, Hannah, tell me about you."

"So that you can pretend to know me?" I startle myself with the question. Confrontation and outward sarcasm aren't really my cup of tea. And speaking with people I haven't known for at least a few months definitely isn't me.

Meli looks slightly offended at first, then her face softens. "Or maybe I actually want to know you." She leans forward, the action drawing my eyes to her face. "Don't worry, I'll tell you all about me, too. I am *quite* interesting." She winks like we're sharing an exciting secret. My heart flips.

"Really?" I lean forward, too. "Tell me, um, something interesting about you, then."

"Okay." The corners of Meli's brown eyes furrow. Then she grins. "Got it. Once, when I was four, I ate a stick of butter."

"Like, in something?"

"No." Meli's grin widens. "With a spoon."

"Wow." I shake my head. "That is gross. Very, very gross. I'm, um, not sure we can be friends."

"Come on, like you've never done something embarrassing."

I scan my mind for something interesting I can tell her. Something about Meli makes me want to talk—even about something embarrassing. Unfortunately, nothing much comes to mind. I live a straightforward life. My dad's military, so we moved around often. Wherever we landed my mom would get very involved in the church, and because of her, I would, too. There was a limited list of activities I could participate in, such as ballet and Bible study. There wasn't a lot of opportunity or time for mischief. When I went to college, I ended up at a large state school I found overwhelming and spent way too much time in my dorm or walking around the nearby forest. I might have been happier at a smaller school, but when my parents pushed me toward their alma mater, it was easier not to argue.

"I've got one." I'm not sure why I'm so willing to share this, but here we go. "And it's more embarrassing because I was older. I started work at McKinnon's right out of college. You know, the company that makes power tools?"

"I know it, but for some reason, I have trouble picturing you with a sandblaster."

"I'm a copywriter." I've loved writing since I was a child, since it was easier than speaking, although writing about power tools isn't exactly fascinating work. "Anyway, on the first day, we had an information session for all the new hires. You know, the endless meetings about company life and our roles and all that. There were a bunch of snacks in the middle of the table. So, I reached for a cookie, and—"

"No fair!" Crystal is back. Her hands are on her hips, and there's an expression of outrage on her pale face. "We're all supposed to get to know Hannah *equally*. Are you angling for maid of honor already?"

My stomach sinks. When we were discussing this plan, Eric told me the bridesmaid who did the best in these first meetings would give the maid of honor speeches and get a bonus. *Maybe Meli was only talking to me for the possible perks, not because she's interested in me as a person.*

"No," Meli says calmly. "I'm angling for *not a bitch*, but I see I won't have any competition from you." She smiles brightly and I don't stifle my laugh in time. Crystal looks at me like I've just grown a second head and flops onto the couch, clearly done with both of us.

After a few minutes, Jen and Charlie arrive with their drinks and sit nearby. Then, as one, they all turn to me. I guess since I'm the reason they're all here, they expect me to do something. My heart starts beating in my chest so fast I'm worried it's going to break my ribs. My breath comes in shorter and shorter gasps. I wish they weren't all staring at me so intently. I wish I weren't here today at all.

A soft hand lands on mine. The touch startles me enough to break my spiral of nerves, and I turn to see Meli's smile. It's encouraging—not like Eric's smile at all. Meli's smile looks real and spontaneous. Her hand feels different from Eric's, too. In a good way.

"Maybe…we can, um, all introduce ourselves?" My voice is a little too quiet, but everyone seems to hear me okay.

"I'll go first," Crystal informs us importantly. "So, I'm Crystal. I'm, like, a model, as you can probably guess." She pauses for a moment to pose by thrusting her chest out. "And I'm also, like, an influencer. So. I'm twenty-three."

"Nice to meet you, Crystal," Meli mutters. Her voice drips with sarcasm. I stifle another giggle.

"Um, I can go next." Charlie stands up, smoothing her skirt and giving us all a friendly smile. I look away before she makes eye contact. Charlie is curvy and pretty, with long braids on one side and sparkling brown eyes. A glance around the circle confirms all the women have long hair and are slim yet curvy. They're all beautiful in a very particular way. My stomach twists. Eric must have picked them for a reason. All these women fit a narrow stereotype of what defines a beautiful woman.

"I'm Charlie," Charlie continues. "I act, but just as a hobby. In my day job, I do admin work at a small law firm."

"Nice to meet you, Charlie." Meli smiles at her encouragingly. Charlie sits back down and Meli's friend stands up. She looks a little less comfortable to be in front of everyone.

"I'm Jen," she says. She nods as though this explains everything and starts to sit again, but Meli nudges her, and she stays on her feet. "Right. So, I'm a web designer. Come to me with all your web design needs, etcetera, etcetera." Everyone smiles.

"I'm Meli," Meli says. Unlike the others, she doesn't stand up, but the fact that she's doing something different doesn't seem to bother her in the least. Meli seems so confident, which is somehow magnetic. "I'm an actor and a drama teacher and now a bridesmaid." She nods at me. Then all eyes turn to me.

"I'm Hannah," I manage. Like Meli, I stay seated. My knees would probably give out if I tried to put any weight on them. "Um, I'm a copywriter."

"Tell us some stories," Crystal suggests. Or perhaps insists. "We need to be ready to talk about you like we know you." She stares at me and waves a hand in a circular motion. Maybe it's not her intention, but I feel pressured to spin an amazing story from thin air. Immediately, my mind goes blank.

"Um…"

"Crystal," Jen sounds a little annoyed. "Give it a rest. Have you never had a conversation with a human being before?"

Meli and Jen exchange eye rolls, which sends a strange stab of longing through me. I look away quickly. I've never been as close with a friend as Meli and Jen seem to be, not since

I was little. As much as I might want a relationship like that, it isn't worth risking again.

"Geez, *sorry* for wanting to do my job well." Crystal rolls her eyes and reaches for her cup and takes a sip, making a face. "Ugh, this is two pumps of caramel when I definitely asked for one and a half!" She shoots a dirty look toward the staff at the counter.

I glance at Meli to see if she's going to comment on this nonsense and she winks at me, her long lashes resting for a second against her cheek before her brown eye bats open again.

The gesture sends a strange feeling straight to my stomach. I panic for a moment about how to respond to the wink, then just turn back to the rest of the group without doing anything. Meli's going to think I'm either aloof or just plain rude. The thought makes my stomach clench in a completely different way, but I try not to let myself care.

After all, Meli's just here because she's being paid to be here.

"Let's play *Never Have I Ever*," Meli suggests. Maybe she's ignoring both Crystal's traumatic caramel pump incident and my odd reaction to her wink. "We all have drinks, and we need to get to know each other, right?"

"How do you play?"

Crystal sighs as though my not knowing this game is the most terrible thing ever, but Meli doesn't seem to mind.

"Simple. I say something that I've never done like *never have I ever been engaged*. If you *have* done it, you take a drink. Whoever empties their cup last wins."

I am totally going to win this game. I've hardly done anything interesting, and my mug is still almost full. I obediently raise my cup of hot chocolate to take a sip. So does Charlie.

"I'm actually married." She lifts her hand to display a simple gold wedding band and toasts us with her chai.

"Okay, so I'm next," Jen says. I'm relieved. I don't have

to go next. Though now I have more time to worry about what I'm going to say while all the other women take a turn. *Oh, the struggles of being horribly, socially anxious*. "Never have I ever performed in a circus as a trapeze artist."

"Hey!" Meli shakes her head. "I feel like that was targeted at me."

"It was," Jen says. "Drink!"

Meli takes a long sip, but no one else does. "I've performed in a bunch of different troupes, including one that focused on physical theatre like trapeze and aerial silks. I wouldn't call it a *circus* exactly, but there you go."

Charlie bites her lip. "I think I can get all of you," she says. "Never have I ever eaten peanuts. At least not that I remember." She grins when we all take a drink. "I'm allergic."

"Okay," Crystal says. "So, like, never have I ever eaten vanilla ice cream."

I'm impressed she thought of something so universal that we all drank. And it wasn't even offensive.

"Why not?" Charlie asks. "I mean, vanilla isn't the best flavor, but it's not the worst."

"I don't know. I just never tried it. There are just so many other flavors and that one seems so…boring." Crystal shrugs. "Hannah, your turn."

"Um, okay." I tug on a strand of my hair, trying to think of something. My heart is beating fast, but I take deep breaths, forcing myself to stay calm. "Never have I ever sung in front of people."

Crystal, Meli, Jen, and Charlie all drink.

"I just sang as part of some play back in school," Jen says. "And it was so bad that the director told me to sing more quietly. Back to you, Meli."

"Never have I ever been a bridesmaid before," Meli suggests. No one drinks except me. "Darn, I felt good about that one. I thought I'd get more people."

"Never have I ever slept with a woman," Jen says next.

"Come on, I feel like you're only going after me," Meli complains with a smile. She takes another sip.

"Maybe it's just because I know I can get you to drink every time and I don't know any of these other people very well." Jen grins.

While they're all talking, I take a quick sip, too. Unfortunately, Crystal notices. *Why couldn't she have been distracted by her caramel pumps or her nails or something equally frivolous?*

"Wait a minute," she says, looking between Meli and me. "Her, I get." She points one finger at Meli. "She's clearly into women. But you? You're engaged to a man!"

"Wow," Meli says, shaking her head. "You can't tell who might be interested in whom just by looking at them."

"And you shouldn't try," Jen adds. She tosses her hair over her shoulder.

"Come on," Crystal protests, looking at Charlie as though she might have an ally. "I was just saying—"

"Well, don't say that." Charlie gives her a too polite smile, looking tense and on edge, and Meli leans across the coffee table to offer another fist bump. I guess the one she gave me wasn't special.

"Let's move along," Meli concludes, relaxing back into her seat again.

"Okay, never have I ever gone skinny-dipping," Charlie says. Her slim shoulders have relaxed a little. Jen, Meli, and Crystal all drink. Of course, I don't drink. The idea of skinny-dipping has never even occurred to me.

"I think I go skinny-dipping more than regular swimming," Crystal informs us. I want to make a comment about how *grateful* we are to know this fascinating detail, but, of course, I don't.

"I've only been once," Jen says. "With Meli."

"Oh yeah!" Meli's eyes light up at the memory. "It was our first year in college and we jumped in that lake."

"It was a terrible idea." Jen laughs. "Some yucky slimy lake plant touched my leg and I thought there was a monster in the water."

"The only saving grace is that it was nighttime and there was no one around to hear you screaming your head off," Meli concludes.

"My turn," Crystal says, a little abruptly. "Never have I ever *not* slept with the man I'm engaged to marry in, like, a month." She turns to me, eyes keen with interest. "Come on, Hannah. We're supposed to get to know you, and this is juicy. Are you super religious, or something?"

Everyone's eyes are on me, and my face is burning. Meli, Jen, and Charlie look ready to leap to my defense, but this is just too much. My heart is racing. I need to think. I need to go. I jump to my feet, accidentally knocking the coffee table with my shin, and hustle out of the café, not even pausing to get my bag or rain jacket from the coat rack at the door. It's the wrong thing to do in almost any social situation, but I just can't think of a single response, and I have no interest in sitting there stammering until I figure one out or they all give up.

It's raining the cold and misty rain that makes Portland famous. I'm instantly cold and I'm not sure where I'm going, which is not ideal, especially since I don't have my jacket or purse. But I just can't face going back into that café and dealing with Crystal, the World's Worst Fake Bridesmaid.

We're in the Hawthorne district, which is a good hour walk from Eric's Pearl District condo, but luckily only about fifteen minutes from my studio apartment. Unfortunately, without my key, the most I can do is to try to slip into the lobby of my building and wait for someone to rescue me.

I'm going to have to go back into the café to get my things. My heart sinks at the realization. I don't want to face those women again. Or, at least, I don't want to face Crystal. The thought of it makes my stomach hurt, but I don't really have a choice. I start the deep breathing exercises that a YouTube video suggested to prepare to go back inside.

"Hey." I turn to see Meli emerge from the café alone. She wears her raincoat, but the hood is open, and her dark hair is misted with droplets of rain. She still looks gorgeous. "I thought you might want these." She holds out my purse in one hand and my raincoat in the other. I slip the coat on and zip it against the cold, pull the hood up over my already-wet hair, and then take my purse.

"Thanks."

"I bet you want to get home…But if you want to talk or something, I'm here."

Meli looks a little unsure for the first time since I watched her walk into the café. Maybe she's trying to decide if she should just quit this job. I wouldn't blame her, although the thought of her bailing makes me want to curl up and cry. The only part of this little café-based interrogation that was pleasant was Meli. Without her, as nice as Jen and Charlie seem, they're just a bunch of new strangers. I shrug.

"I better get home."

"Of course." Meli smiles, but the expression doesn't quite reach her eyes. I'm about to turn away when I see that she's biting her lip. I turn back. I'm very familiar with the struggle of indecision, and I hate when people rush me. I want to give her plenty of time to decide how she wants to proceed.

"Look," she says, "I'm probably being way too pushy here, but I really would like to talk. Have a real conversation. I'd like to get to know you and I don't think that's going to happen in a group like that. I know a great brunch place literally a block from here and I haven't eaten yet. Maybe you have. But then you could have a piece of cake. They also do some good desserts. It's still pretty early—or maybe you have lunch plans later. I guess really what I'm saying is that if you don't mind, I want to keep hanging out."

I'm smiling again. It seems Meli's nerves have the opposite effect on her than mine have on me. She gets *ramble-y* instead of going silent like I do.

"What about Jen?" I ask. Meli glances back at the café and I follow her gaze to where Jen and Charlie stand under the awning in front of Crystal. From the way they're standing next to each other, arms crossed, the conversation doesn't seem pleasant.

"I told her we'd meet up later," Meli says.

"Then okay."

"Okay?" Meli's eyes widen, and I swear they light up a little. "Okay to brunch?"

"Yeah."

"Great!" She smiles at me as she leads the way down the rainy street.

Nerves and excitement are at war in my stomach as we walk to the café. I've just agreed to continue this social interaction. As nervous as I am, I can't bring myself to regret my decision. I'm too excited at the prospect of spending a little more time with Meli.

CHAPTER THREE

I'm pretty sure I've made a terrible mistake.

Once, when I was a teenager, I crushed on a straight friend. *Emma.* She was very, very straight. She was dating Mark, a nerdy guy from our class who she said was the best kisser she'd ever kissed. He had been cast in the role of best kisser, I thought, mostly because he was her only experience at the time. Still, I was pretty sure Emma was interested in me, too. She left little clues. One day, she wore a pair of socks with a subtle rainbow around the top. Another time, she told me I was one of her favorite people. And sometimes, during sleepovers, we would cuddle to watch scary movies and she would hold my hand.

It was all fairly normal friend stuff, really, but at the time, I was certain it meant she felt for me the same way I felt for her. I was so sure that I asked her to prom. Luckily for both of us, it was when we were alone together, and she took it as a joke. She went to prom with her boyfriend, and I went for a solo hike on Mount Hood.

It took me a long time to get over Emma. I swore I was never going to let myself crush on a straight girl again. And for almost a decade, I haven't.

Yet here I am. I have a terrible sense of déjà vu, like I've seen this exact scene before. Hannah is fascinating—endearingly awkward, beautiful, and clearly a nerd like I am if our Harry Potter conversation is any indication. She's never slept with the man she's supposed to marry. I'm burning with curiosity about that one, although I'm not going to be a Crystal about it.

Still, some part of me says that maybe she hasn't slept with Eric because she doesn't want to. Maybe she's not that into him. After all, people don't always get married because they love each other. Maybe she hasn't slept with him because she's religious. Or maybe she has perfectly valid reasons that are none of my business. Or maybe…she could be into women.

"Is the special good?" Hannah pulls me from my reverie. I've been staring at the menu I've read a thousand times.

"Yes. The tofu scramble is to die for. Oh, it's all vegetarian here. I hope that's okay."

"That's okay." She peruses the menu for a few more minutes. "I think I'll have the Sunrise Scramble."

"That's my favorite." Just like when I first saw her, a little bell dings in my head and tells me this girl is awesome. *Stupid bell.* "You can't go wrong with hash browns, veggie sausage, scrambled tofu, cheese, mushrooms, bell peppers, and guac. Oh, but you might want to ask for it without the jalapenos if you don't like spicy food. It can get a little hot."

"I love spicy food." *Of course you do, Hannah.* Of course.

"Meli in the house!" The waiter, Mak, sidles over, doing a little dance. Mak, and my friendship with him, are the two biggest draws of this restaurant. He knows me, my regular order, and more than a few sordid tales from my life. He even attends most of my performances, standing out from the crowd with his spiky pink hair and tattoo sleeves.

"Good morning to you, too." I extend a fist bump, which he returns with an explosion sound effect.

"The usual?"

"You got it."

"And for your much lovelier companion?" He turns to

Hannah. The small smile she wore as she decided on her food immediately disappears and her whole face pales. Since she's fairly pale already, the drain of color is a little scary. She opens her mouth, then closes it with her eyes wide.

"You wanted the Sunrise Scramble, too, right?" I am unable to let her suffer like this. Hannah nods.

"And something to drink?" Mak asks kindly. He's modulated his voice to be less boisterous and more subdued. Maybe he sees Hannah's discomfort like I did. Hannah shakes her head, and he bustles toward the kitchen.

"I should have asked for some juice." Hannah watches the door through which Mak disappeared seconds before. My heart goes out to her. "I wish I weren't this…awkward."

"You aren't awkward." We just met, but no one can talk about themselves like that in front of me no matter how long I've known them. "At least *awkward* isn't how I'd put it. It doesn't seem like you're just shy or not chatty. It seems like it's very stressful for you to talk to people."

"Yeah. Talking to people is…hard." Hannah looks down. "I don't know if it's shyness or something else. It's just…hard." She reaches for the sugar packets. After a few more moments of silence, I realize she is building some kind of structure. I guess she's not interested in discussing her people-related difficulties further. I reach for the little tubs of creamer and get to work on a moat. Hannah visibly relaxes as we build together. Her pink lips curve into a slight smile as she grabs the salt and pepper shakers to use as turrets on either side.

"What should we call it?" She gestures to the behemoth we've created. Pink Sweet'N Low packets form the outside wall, with a toothpick-and-napkin flag stuck into the top of the pepper shaker to mark the territory. My moat has morphed into more of a high wall around the castle, although it is connected with a Stevia drawbridge.

"Terabithia, maybe."

Hannah's small nose wrinkles. "Really? I always hated that book."

"Yeah." I straighten the drawbridge. "Me too, but the name is pretty. Honestly, a lot of those older kids' books are just depressing. *Where the Red Fern Grows* is bad, too."

"The dog always dies," Hannah shakes her head, "or one of the kids. It's like they were trying to make a whole generation depressed and worried about their pets and their friends and their own health."

"True!" I laugh a little. "My mom grew up on French children's books, which I think are equally bad, but a little more artsy."

"Your mom is French?"

"Yes. And my dad is Indian. But they met here in the States in college."

"In Portland?"

"No, in Massachusetts. But they moved here because my dad read an article on the *Best Cities in the US for Quality of Living*." I include air quotes around the name of the article. Hannah grins. "After debating the best of the best options, they picked Portland."

"How romantic. Yet also practical."

"Indeed. But my parents really *are* romantic. They're very much in love, even after more than thirty years together."

"That's sweet."

"And they're fine with me being a lesbian." As I say the words, I look at the table. Part of me worries she really *is* religious. If she is, she might end this brunch before it even begins, which would be quite a blow. If Hannah doesn't accept my sexuality, I'll probably step back from the wedding party, the ten thousand dollars forgotten. Or I'll just go and try to avoid her. Ten thousand dollars is a lot of money.

I glance at Hannah to see her reaction.

"They sound like cool people." Hannah maneuvers the flag

on the castle as though searching for an invisible breeze. She seems completely unfazed by my revelation. "Do they still live in Portland?"

"No." I smile, but I'm a little sad that I have no family here anymore. "They retired last year and decided they wanted to live somewhere warm, so they're in Mexico now. But I visit them often and they visit me." I pause. "What about your parents?"

The food arrives before Hannah can answer. It's steaming and smells delicious. Hannah's whole face lights up. I smile, too, even though I've eaten this dish at least fifty times. It just never gets old.

"Could we also get some juice?" I ask Mak as he sets my plate on the table.

"Of course. We have fresh-squeezed orange juice today," Mak says. I look at Hannah and she nods slightly, now biting her lip.

"Perfect," I tell Mak. "Two glasses, please."

I unfold my napkin into my lap and reach for my fork, but I pause before eating so I can gauge Hannah's reaction to the food. Hannah loads her fork with a little bit of everything. After chewing for a moment, she sighs a little sigh of pleasure. My heart tumbles over itself. I'm not disappointed I waited to start eating if that sound was my reward. *Not at all.*

"My parents," she says after she finishes chewing, "are Chad, who's in the Air Force, and Jana, who is a homemaker. They're nice people, but they're always on the move. They're in North Dakota now."

"Are they coming to your wedding?" She nods.

"My parents and my brother, Brad, are all coming. And I think some assorted cousins."

I'm a little surprised Hannah doesn't know who from her family will come to the wedding. But I've realized something else that quickly moves me forward.

"Hold on. Your dad's name is Chad and your brother is…"

"Brad." Hannah rolls her eyes a little. "And my mom's name is Jana and I'm Hannah."

I burst out laughing. I can't help it. I hope she doesn't think I'm making fun of her, because I'm not, but it's just too funny. I had no idea people really named their kids like that. Luckily, Hannah doesn't seem offended at all.

"How about Meli?" she asks once I've regained my composure and resumed my meal. "Where's that from?"

I quickly swallow my current bite. "Meli is short for Amelie."

"Pretty." She smiles and my heart flutters. *Stupid heart.* This is going to be a disaster.

"Thanks." I turn my attention back to my food, but I'm still thinking about the upcoming disaster.

If Jen were here, she would tell me to stop mooning over Hannah, and to go out with her friend Susan. Jen's been trying to set me up with Susan for about five years now. Jen isn't here, though, because I left her behind at the café with barely a backward glance.

"Are you looking forward to Saint Sofia?" Hannah asks. Saint Sofia is the private Caribbean resort island where her wedding will take place. *Stupid wedding.*

"Yes," I say. *Well, that is half true and half a blatant lie.* "I've never been to the Caribbean, so it should be fun." The wedding will be fun, but the actual marriage-slash-Eric part is less exciting. "Hey, if your wedding is on a private island, where's the honeymoon?"

Hannah's nose wrinkles again. "No honeymoon yet. Eric needs to get back to work soon after the wedding, so there isn't really time. But the wedding festivities are going to last a whole week, so that's basically better than a honeymoon."

She doesn't sound like she believes what she said, especially given the slightly mocking tone in which she said that last bit, but I'm not going to push. Even if some terrible part of me wants to find the cracks in her future marriage and apply pressure. I'm way too eager to find any evidence that she deserves better than her groom.

Think of Emma and the disaster that was, you fool. I don't really care about the wedding or the honeymoon, and certainly not Eric. Maybe it's time for a change of topic.

"So, what books do you like, apart from Harry Potter? I already know that you're not into books where the dog dies."

Hannah appears thoughtful. "I like most books, really. Well, I tend to steer clear of anything too depressing or cerebral."

"Oh, me too! Books are my time to escape the world around me, not to deal with the *despairs of the human soul* or whatever." I use a dramatic voice for emphasis and Hannah laughs. "That's why I act, too."

"What kind of plays do you do?"

"Different things. My performance group, Gingersnap Company, reimagines fairy tales from around the world, which is fun. I also help run a youth troupe called the Kew Kids. They usually create their own themes, so they do a bunch of narratives about identity and belonging and love. And then I perform in other plays, classics like Shakespeare." I'm worried that I'm rambling, but Hannah still looks interested.

"What's your favorite?"

I consider her question. "I'm not sure. I did a really fun physical theatre play with lots of acrobatics. I love how much emotion I can convey with a flick of the wrist or a dynamic tumbling sequence or a suspenseful drop on fabric. And it's fun to move my body that way. I loved that experience, but I think all the plays have something going for them. Or most of them, anyway. I acted in this one terrible play about the fracturing of a marriage that I just hated."

"That does sound dreadful. Last week, Eric dragged me to a film about economic downturns and the deterioration of the concept of collaboration. He said it was amazing because it was critically acclaimed, but I honestly would have rather watched some kids' movie."

I shudder. "I can't stand movies about economics or war or anything like that. They're always so slow and moody. Anyway. What would you have wanted to watch instead?"

"I kind of love animated movies?" Hannah ends the sentence like a question. "Like, Disney animation, but also Miyazaki movies."

"What's that?"

"Miyazaki is a Japanese animator who creates these really great, imaginative movies. There's one, *Spirited Away*, that I watched about a hundred times as a kid. I always felt like it held the secrets to life. And the animation was awesome."

"I've never seen one, but I'd like to. Maybe you can show me one." *Oh.* I probably shouldn't have suggested that. I'm still not sure what kind of situations Hannah finds stressful. Plus, she's getting married soon, and I'm not sure if she'll want to spend time with me after that. Hannah nods, though.

"Okay." There's a moment of silence as we both eat.

"Have you ever been in a play?" I ask.

"Just once, in elementary school. My class put on a play. I got so flustered trying to say my lines they demoted me to the part of a non-talking tree."

"There's always a tree in these things. I played a non-talking tree in an elementary school play, too."

"Really? Why didn't you have a speaking role? You're such a good actor."

"You don't know that." I wiggle my eyebrows and Hannah blushes.

"I guess not. But I saw how confident you were in the café, and you just seemed…"

I wait for her to finish the thought before I realize she's not going to.

"Thanks, then. Anyway, my teacher thought I was a bit of a drama queen who was always trying to steal the spotlight, so she demoted me. Maybe it was true, but I was just a kid. My mom *had words* with her later. Anyway, it's nice to meet a fellow tree. What kind of tree were you?"

"I never thought about it. Probably a maple or something. You?"

"I was definitely a weeping willow." I hold my arms out from my sides with my hands pointing down like the branches of a willow. "I also kept dancing and making noises in the background. That probably didn't help my argument that I was *not* a drama queen and that I *didn't* want to steal the spotlight." I laugh aloud.

"We are such different people. When I was a tree, I tried my absolute best to not move at all so no one would notice me." She holds her arms up in a frozen tableau of a tree, then sweeps her eyes back and forth with pretend worry.

"That is a very excellent tree. Speaking of embarrassing experiences, what was the end of that cookie story from earlier?"

"Right! Okay, so it was my first day at a new job, and I saw that plate of cookies and snacks in the middle of the table. I reached over—" Her phone rings and her eyes widen before she looks down at it. I get the impression that phone calls are anxiety-provoking for her.

"Eric." She swipes to answer and holds the phone to her ear. I can't make out words, but I can hear the sound of the voice on the other end. He sounds annoyed. Finally, Eric falls silent, and Hannah says, "I'm sorry, it was just so many people and"—there's a blast of tinny squeaking from Eric—"Yes, of course… um, y-you're right. Okay. S-sorry."

She drops the phone on the table with an audible *smack* and runs her hands over her face and down the length of her hair, tucking it behind her ears.

"Uh…Everything okay?" It's obvious that it isn't, but I want her to know she can talk to me. I want to comfort her if I can.

"Not really." She shrugs half-heartedly and adds an unconvincing smile that looks more like a grimace. "Eric's unhappy I left like that. He reminded me how embarrassing it would be if anyone were to find out that I didn't have real friends and had to hire my bridesmaids."

"He sounds like a bit of a jerk." *Classy, Meli.*

Hannah shakes her head. "No, no. He's trying to help me. Us."

Himself.

"I just wish I could hold it together a little better in these situations," Hannah continues. "Anyway, I better head home. I guess I'll see you for the bachelorette party."

Hannah leaves a twenty on the table over my protest, grabs her coat, and hurries away. I stare at my almost empty plate while my stomach churns. I have half a mind to chase her again, but there's only so many times anyone can do that in one day without being creepy. Instead, I watch her hurry away, her head bowed, her gray hood pulled over her hair.

I hate that Eric makes Hannah feel like her social anxiety is her fault. Frankly, I hate him for leaving her alone with the four of us in the first place, even though that led to us meeting. For some inexplicable reason, it seems Hannah does want to marry him, though.

My college girlfriend Kami was distant with most people and could seem standoffish, but when we were alone together, she was hilarious and thoughtful. Eric might be like that. Kami was never rude or belittling the way Eric is, though. Hannah doesn't seem to realize how demeaning he is to her. Maybe Eric has a sweet or funny side he just hasn't shown yet. Or maybe Hannah has other reasons for wanting to get married which are, again, none of my business.

I can fight it as much as I want. I can remind myself of Emma. I can recite over and over that getting in the way of other people's relationships is never wise. I can try to like Eric. It isn't going to matter.

I want Hannah to see how amazing she is. I want her to be with someone who doesn't belittle her or put her in situations that clearly make her uncomfortable. And if the journey ends with Hannah not getting married—well, maybe that would be for the best.

Chapter Four

I'm not mad," Eric assures me, probably for the hundredth time today. He curls an arm around me and pulls me in close. "I just wish you would try harder."

"I am trying. Really, I am." We're sitting on the couch in his condo with a blanket over our laps. This is my favorite time with Eric. He seems to soften around the edges when we're alone like this. It's only when we're around other people and my long pauses and whispered answers get on his nerves that he's a little prickly.

"I know, sweetheart." He kisses the top of my head, then very gently tilts my head back and presses a kiss to my lips. When he pulls away, he has a familiar expectant, eager expression on his face. He's more excited about the wedding than I am—and he's particularly excited about what will come the night after. "Only two more weeks."

I smile, but my heart squeezes. I told him right after we met that my parents had raised me to be very religious and I wouldn't want to have sex before marriage. That was probably why he proposed so fast, just two months after the night that we sat in a corner of my office holiday party—hosted at one of his hotels—and talked for hours. He decided President's Day was the most romantic of all holidays for a proposal, and I was surprised and flattered enough to say yes, and here we are.

Still, I'm beyond nervous about sleeping with him, even though I don't have any religious qualms about it. My parents would probably encourage it. They're okay with whatever it takes to get me into a stable, married relationship with a man.

Kissing is…fine. It isn't great, though. There's no reason to think sex would be any better—and the thought of sex with any man makes my stomach clench.

I give myself an internal shake. It will be better. It must be better because Eric and I will be together forever. There is no going back. If I got a divorce, it would shatter my very religious and traditional family. Plus, there's not much of a chance I would ever get up the nerve to say I wanted a divorce if I did.

It's too early to think about divorce, of course. We're not even married yet.

It's been nearly a week since the disastrous bridesmaids' coffee chat. Eric was annoyed with me when I got to his house that evening, but he forgave me quickly. He always does.

Today the wish for me to try harder is about something else. There's a formal dinner with investors tomorrow night. He wants me to go.

I would rather sink into a large hole full of spiders.

"Just try," he says softly. He's sure his kiss has softened me and that I'll say yes now. He's just that confident, even though his kisses don't do a lot for me. I admire that confidence. "Come on. There's going to be a performance by some local kids, some fresh-caught Pacific salmon…You'll love it. And I'll be right there the whole time."

"Okay." I give in. It's the right thing to do. After all, I should support him when I can. Hopefully there will be some nice side dishes for the salmon—I don't like fish. Eric loves salmon, and my quiet suggestions that I don't have fallen on deaf ears. I stopped trying to get it removed from my menu. *Just another example of my inability to speak up for myself.*

"Thank you, sweetheart." Eric leans in to kiss me on the cheek. "It's going to be so much fun. I promise."

❖

And this is how I find myself laced into a strappy blue dress and sitting between Eric and one of his business contacts at dinner the next night. We've been here for half an hour, and I already want to leave. There are so many people who want to talk to Eric and me and congratulate us on our wedding. It's extremely overwhelming. If this is how it's going to be at our actual wedding, I'd better make a nice home for myself in that spider pit.

"Before we get started on the meal," the MC for the night, Amanda something, announces, "we have a performance from a youth drama troupe, the Kew Kids!"

The Kew Kids. That sounds familiar. I turn toward the front of the room, where a small stage has been erected and obscured by thick black curtains. When the curtains open, I see a girl maybe eleven or twelve years old standing in the center of the stage. She's wearing a flowy blue dress, and one hand is stretched toward the ceiling.

"I feel so alone here." Her voice trembles. She turns toward the audience, hands dropping to her sides. "Does anyone know where I am?"

For a minute or so, she traverses the stage alone, reciting a monologue about how she came to be lost all alone in a strange forest. When Eric leans to whisper something to me, I whack him none too gently on the arm. I want to hear the performance.

Then a rush of ten or so children and teenagers swarms the stage. They're all talking over each other, laughing, and they pick the girl up and draw her in. The awe on her face is striking, even though I know it's just for show. Then the whole group starts…it's not dancing, really. It's more climbing on each other, like each kid is a piece of playground equipment or a tree branch. Some of the smaller actors get thrown from one side of the stage to the other, causing the whole audience to gasp. They twirl together and apart, forming pictures with their bodies. I thought acting was all nonspeaking trees and old stuffy Shakespeare, not beautiful pictures and sweeping emotions like this.

At the end, the girl and one of the older boys have a few more lines about how the girl will go with them now. Then they sweep off the stage to thunderous applause.

"That was amazing," I say aloud. Eric looks surprised at my strong opinion, but he smiles.

"I always hire this troupe for my events," he says. "There's nothing like cute kids and drama to get people invested." *Of course, it has to be about lining his pockets, not about supporting local arts.*

"Hmm." I look to where the performers are streaming into a side hallway. "I'm going to congratulate them."

"You're going to willingly talk to people?" Eric teases. "All right, then. Just be back soon. I think the appetizers are next."

I politely excuse myself in a hushed murmur, and wind between the tables toward the side door. I follow a teenager through. They're all congratulating each other, complete with high fives, fist bumps, and excited voices comparing the best parts of the piece. I'm instantly out of place. These kids are a team, a community. They don't need my congratulations on their work. I'm about to slip back into the dining room when someone catches my arm.

"Hannah?"

I turn in surprise.

"Meli?"

"What are you doing here?" She grins broadly.

"This is Eric's event," I say. "Didn't you speak with him when you were organizing your performance?"

"No, only an assistant. So, what did you think?"

I shake my head in wonder. "Amazing. Is this the kind of theatre that you do?"

"Sometimes." Meli grins modestly. "Like I told you, I'm a member of a few local performance troupes. Some of them are physical theatre, like you saw, and others are more straight-up acting. Anyway, maybe you can see now why I love physical theatre so much."

"Meli!" The young girl who performed the beginning monologue scampers over, breathing hard. "Did you see the thigh stand sequence? It was so perfect!" She catches sight of me. "Oh, hi."

"Hi." I smile at her. Kids are always easier to talk to than adults. "That was fantastic. You all are very talented."

"Thanks." She bobs a cute little bow. "Are you Meli's friend?"

"Yes." It seems to be the simplest explanation. "Meli is actually my bridesmaid."

"Oh, you're the one who's getting married. Hannah. Cool!" The girl scampers away to her friends and Meli turns to me, her cheeks a shade darker than usual.

"It wasn't that I told them about you per se," Meli explains. "I just told them I'd be gone for a week, and you know kids. They had lots of questions."

"It's okay. It's sweet she likes you so much."

Meli grins.

"Thanks. I love these kids."

"Do you need to go and, um, chaperone them?" I'm not sure exactly how much kids this age need looking after. They seem pretty self-sufficient, but I don't want to make assumptions.

"Yes, I need to stick with them until their parents pick them up or the older ones head off home. But we could meet after? I should be done in an hour or so."

I pause to consider the unexpected invitation. Eric and I should be finished with dinner in an hour and then on to the mingling portion of events—my least favorite part. Maybe I can mingle with Meli instead. Talking to her is easy and natural, just the opposite of how I usually am when talking to people.

"Sounds good. Let's meet back here."

I hurry back into the main dining room. When I reach my seat, Eric seems annoyed based on the look he sends my way. I guess I disappeared for too long.

"That took some time," he points out, confirming my suspicions. His voice is quiet so the people at the tables around us can't hear. "Did you get nervous and freeze?"

"No, I was just talking to one of the coaches. Remember Meli, my bridesmaid? She coaches these kids."

"Hmm…Well, I'm glad you were talking to her, but you missed the appetizer. It was asparagus and salmon puffs."

"Hmm." I hate asparagus and salmon equally and would have struggled through that dish. I could just tell Eric the truth, but I can imagine the look of distaste on his face if he learns that I don't like two of his favorite foods. It's just easier to go along with it. After all, he's going to be my husband. Any successful relationship is all about compromise.

I know I shouldn't have to change myself to be in a relationship. I've seen the same cat posters about *being yourself* and *self-esteem* that everyone else has. However, I've also had to change myself for every significant relationship in my life so far, from my parents to the few friends I was able to cobble together in my youth. It isn't much of a leap to eat some fish now and then—and I can always say I'm not too hungry, then fill up on dessert, as I've done a few times before.

Conversation around the table moves to stock prices and I fiddle with my napkin. I wonder what Meli is doing. Not talking about investments, probably. Not choking down a piece of fish, definitely. I imagine her surrounded by the kids, reliving the performance, probably complimenting them on their work. I smile at the thought of her in her element, her long black hair barely contained by a pink band and her eyes alive with excitement.

Dinner drags on through several courses. I nod and smile at the right times, but no one seems to expect me to talk much. That works for me. My whole life, I've been happiest blending into the background with no one asking me questions. Today, something stings a little, though. I can't forget Meli chatting with me at the café, trying to draw me out. It was nice for someone to attempt to get to know me, and to meet me where I am. Of course, it's too much to ask anyone to do that all the time. But Eric, who knows me best theoretically, could at least remember I'm here and throw me a shared look now and then.

Hush, Hannah. Don't be so critical.

Finally, the last plates are cleared away and I sigh in relief. I hid a large chunk of fish under my napkin and was living in fear someone would notice. Everyone chatters about the lovely meal and gets to their feet to roam toward the standing tables of desserts. I slip toward the side door to meet Meli again. It's been a little more than an hour. Hopefully, she didn't leave.

"What's this?" Eric catches me by the arm as I'm about to extricate myself from the group. I channel the guilt of a misbehaving schoolchild caught by the principal.

"Meli asked me to meet her again after dinner." My voice is quiet.

"Hannah." Eric shakes his head. His smile is condescending. "I know you're new to this world, the world of sophistication, but look around. No one's leaving for any reason. People are going to talk if you run off again."

I do look around. The room is beautifully decorated with tasteful bouquets. The people are beautifully dressed in suits and ties and evening gowns, just like my itchy blue number. The food is beautiful, too. The tiny dessert cakes are decorated with frosting roses and edible pearls and the tiny puddings glisten with shiny chocolate and whipped cream. None of it matters. I don't want to be here. All the people seem fake and supercilious as they laugh their grating little laughs at jokes that aren't funny even while they casually mention their little cottage in Aspen or their weekend villa in Santa Barbara.

I fit with Eric, or I think I do. But I don't fit in here.

Of course, Eric doesn't notice any of this conflict going on inside my head. He just notices I've looked around, as instructed. He reaches for my hand.

"Come on, you aren't going to deny me the opportunity of showing off my beautiful fiancée, are you?"

"Of course not." I smile, though I'm sure it doesn't quite reach my eyes. "But let me go tell Meli I'll see her another time, okay?"

"That sounds very polite." Eric leans in to kiss my cheek. He sometimes chastises me for not being polite enough, so his words are meant to be a compliment. I squeeze his hand, then thread my way through the guests, avoiding eye contact.

Meli sits on a small table in the hallway with one leg crossed. I didn't notice her clothes much before, but in comparison to all the finery inside, her purple yoga pants with crisscrossing threads and her loose black top that shows a glimpse of her smooth stomach stand out. And not in a bad way. When I close the door behind me, she looks up from her phone and her face breaks into a smile.

"Hannah!" She hops gracefully off the table and crosses to me. "How was dinner?"

"Bad." I feel the heat of my flush at my honest answer. "I hate fish, and it seemed like every course featured a different and more disgusting kind of fish."

"Oh no!" Meli looks truly distressed at my predicament. "Didn't they have any other options?"

"I didn't ask."

"Well, either way, that sounds bad indeed. Are you hungry? There's a Burgerville right next door."

Burgerville is a classic Portland fast food joint. When I moved here for college almost seven years ago, a boysenberry milkshake with waffle fries was one of my first meals. Now, the thought of something hot and not fishy sounds tempting, but I promised Eric I'd hurry back.

"I can't." I make a face. "I have to mingle."

"Sure, of course." Meli smiles, but her shoulders have slumped ever so slightly. She's disappointed she can't eat with me. Or, more likely, she's disappointed she might not get fries from Burgerville. It's always hard to tell people's motivations, but it does seem like Meli wants to spend time with me. Otherwise, she'd probably stop inviting me to do stuff with her.

"I need to go." I turn but hesitate with my back to Meli. The door will take me back into the hall, where I'll need to mingle again. And maybe eat a fish dessert. The idea of staying here with Meli is much more appealing.

I can't go to Burgerville *now*, but maybe I can later. My heart starts beating way too fast. I'll see Meli at my bachelorette party next week, and hanging out with her makes me feel… good. Not just about my time, but about myself. When I'm with her, I feel like I'm enough.

"Um, I…how about tomorrow?" I blurt my suggestion before I can lose my nerve. "We could…um…have dinner. Or not." I turn back to see Meli's face, and she beams as if I've offered her a priceless diamond. My heart swells. She might be as excited to spend time with me as I am to spend time with her. I imagine the two of us sharing a milkshake with two straws like in a sixties commercial.

"That would be great. When and where?"

I don't like speaking my mind, because it shows other people what I want and that is scary. They could take my wishes away from me. But today, I barely even hesitate.

"The Burgerville on Twenty-third? Around five thirty?"

"Done." Meli nods. "I have a rehearsal near there until five. I should be on time, but if I'm late, rehearsal ran over. Also, maybe you could give me your number, just in case something goes wrong?"

"Okay." We exchange numbers and Meli sails off with a wave and a little bounce in her step. My heart lifts. I finally have her number, something I never thought to ask for. It's been a while since someone seemed so interested in spending time with me.

Even Eric seems more interested in what I can do for him than in just getting to know me. He wants to have a young, pretty wife on his arm; someone to lend him a little gravitas and be his plus-one for parties. He doesn't necessarily need that young, pretty wife to have her own thoughts about things. *Shush, Hannah.*

Still, there's a bounce in my step, too, as I head back into the dining room. I can manage a little mingling tonight if tomorrow I get to share a milkshake with Meli.

Spending time with Meli doesn't grate on me, even though spending time with anyone else, even Eric, does. I try not to question that fact too much. That's not the kind of thing a soon-to-be married woman should really be thinking about.

Chapter Five

"So, you're disappearing on us for a week."

I sit on the edge of the stage with Ryan, one of my closest friends in Gingersnap Company. We're waiting, juice boxes in hand, for another scene to wrap so we can go home. I can't stop glancing at my phone to see the time, not wanting to be late for my dinner with Hannah, but I tuck the device into my pocket now and turn my full attention to Ryan like the good friend I try to be.

"Indeed."

He shakes his head dramatically while he takes another sip of juice. "I think we'll fall apart without you."

Gingersnap Company is my great love in the theatre world. Ryan, Shin, Maria, and I started the company almost five years ago, all still fresh to the world of theatre and performance and all excited to tell classic stories with a twist. I make my money from teaching kids and acting in professional companies or the occasional advertisement, but I get my professional fulfillment from Gingersnap Company.

Right now, we're telling a version of *Hansel and Gretel* set in modern-day China. Shin is the director, but we're all involved. And thanks to a stroke of luck, we'll get to perform at a few prominent festivals across the state this summer.

"Nah, you'll be fine. I'm not in that many scenes."

Ryan gives me a bit of side-eye at that comment. "You're Gretel."

I shrug. *Sure, I'm Gretel, but now I'm a bridesmaid, too.* The roles aren't exactly compatible, but they're both in my range.

"So, tell me, what could be so important as to abandon us?" Ryan slurps the last of his juice box, which makes me shudder, and tosses it easily into the trash can. In his spare time, Ryan plays basketball and does some freelance coding. He's one of those rare people who was popular with nerds, jocks, *and* theatre folk in high school.

"I'm going to a wedding." I take a daintier sip of the remainder of my juice box and manage to toss it into the trash can on the first try. Ryan claps and I take a bow. "On a private island in the Caribbean. White sand, tropical beaches…I have to say, it'll be a lot more fun than looking at your sorry face."

"Wow." Ryan draws out the word while he shakes his head. "*Rude*. Who's getting married, anyway? I thought I knew most of your friends."

"You do." I lean back against the edge of the chair I'm sitting in front of. Eric made me sign an NDA about the whole wedding situation, so I can't exactly give away the ending here. "The bride, Hannah, is a newer friend."

"But she still asked you to be her bridesmaid?" Ryan raises his eyebrows.

"Yeah. Well. I just have that kind of magnetic personality." I wink at him. Part of me wishes I could spill the whole story to Ryan about how much I like Hannah and how she's getting married, but it's probably for the best that I'm not legally allowed to. It's more than a little embarrassing.

Only a few more minutes pass before Shin claps his hands and dismisses us. I'm a bit late, but Burgerville isn't far away. As I wave good-bye to my fellow cast members, I break into a quick walk, enjoying the crisp spring air and the smell of rain. It's still a bit chilly, but a few buds have started to grow on the trees, and a couple of hearty flowers have already stubbornly pushed their way out of the damp soil. Not long has passed since the first meeting at the café, but the weather is already less miserable here.

I arrive at Burgerville just as Hannah does. She wears her gray raincoat again and her head is bowed. I wonder what she's thinking about with that solemn expression. Maybe I can cheer her up with a witty comment—or maybe I should just get her attention.

"Hey!" I call out with a wave.

When she sees me, she straightens and smiles. "Hey, yourself."

She hugs me. The gesture is so surprising I almost step back. Then I wrap my arms around her, and for a moment, we're pressed against each other, raincoats crinkling. We're nearly the same height and my nose is pressed against the side of her head. Her hair smells like cinnamon.

I quickly end the embrace, letting my hands fall to my sides. Hannah doesn't seem to notice I've been sniffing her hair. *That's a relief.* She just steps to the side and opens the door of the Burgerville, then waves me in like I'm an important lady. I fall easily into the role and play the part with a little flounce. She laughs softly.

Disaster looms. I already like her so much and her wedding is so close and her hair smells like cinnamon. Too many thoughts whirl through my head.

"What are you going to order?" I try to get back on stable footing.

"I can never decide." She shrugs and gives a self-deprecating smile. "I love the chocolate milkshakes, but the boysenberry milkshakes are a classic. And I'm torn between the waffle fries and the onion rings, as usual."

"We could order all of the above and share."

"Yes." Hannah wiggles like a happy little puppy. "I love it. Um, do you mind ordering?"

"No problem." I go to the counter to place the order and meet her a few minutes later at a window booth with our number 16 on its little plastic number stand. I can't take it anymore. I have to know.

"So, tell me the story."

"The story?" Hannah looks confused. "What story?"

"You know." I make a little hand-flipping gesture as if collecting whisps of a story from the air. "The story of how you and Eric fell in love. That annoying little story that makes everyone who isn't part of a couple want to die."

"Um, okay." Hannah shifts in her chair. "Well…you know I'm a copywriter at McKinnon's. Last year, we had our Christmas party at one of Eric's hotels. I was standing in the corner by myself, trying to look casual and waiting until I could leave." She rolls her eyes. "Then Eric spotted me. I don't know why, but he came right over. I was terrified, but he was friendly, and I didn't have to worry about talking much, because he was super chatty. We ended up hanging out the whole evening."

"Do your parents like him?"

Hannah snorts.

"*Like* him? That's not a strong enough word. I think they love him more than me at this point. Honestly, this is all they've ever wanted for me. They want to see me married to a"—she makes air quotes—"*good* man who can provide for us both."

I think I'm starting to see what happened here. Hannah's been told her whole life that marriage was the endgame, so when it was offered, she couldn't or wouldn't say no. There's a lot I still don't know, but the more that comes together of this story, the surer I am that her wedding is a mistake.

"And you're happy?" I force the words out. If she says yes, I'll trust her word. I'm going to make myself give up on this quest. Eric might suck, but Hannah is a grown woman, and she can make her own decisions. I can't ruin her wedding because I think she deserves better. I have to respect her and her decisions. I can remove myself from the situation. Maybe I'll call in sick to the wedding. Maybe I'll back out. But only if she says she's happy.

But she doesn't say yes. She hesitates with her lips slightly parted, and there's a long pause. Then she laughs again. It's another short, false-sounding laugh.

"Why wouldn't I be happy? This is what I've always wanted."

And it's enough. My traitorous heart hears her words and feels a spark of hope. She doesn't sound happy. As selfish or as misguided as it might be, there's still a chance to make Hannah realize that she deserves better. Even if her better choice isn't me, since she probably is straight.

Probably, but not definitely.

Shut up, stupid heart.

"Anyway, how about you? Any girlfriend?" The drinks and fries arrive, and Hannah takes a deep inhale and smiles. I can't overstate how attractive she is when she enjoys something.

"No." I reach for the chocolate milkshake, trying to appear casual, and almost poke my eye out with the straw. I finally manage a sip with no eye-related injuries. "Not at the moment."

"And, um, historically?"

"Are you really interested in my love life?"

Hannah slides the chocolate milkshake from my hand and takes a long drink. Of course, I can't help thinking how we're using the same straw and that it is almost like our mouths are touching.

Great—now I'm a lovesick teenager.

"Sure I am." Hannah gently lifts the lid from the shake. "I, um, I don't know many lesbians."

I'm not sure what to say. I hate when people ask about my

romantic history because they're looking for some saucy stories they can tell their other friends to show how open-minded they are. But her earnest expression makes her interest seem genuine, and I am not about to quash her curiosity.

"Well, I had a girlfriend in college. Kami. We were together for about a year. But since then, nothing serious."

She nods thoughtfully and reaches for another fry.

I don't really want to admit I've spent the last few years playing the field. Portland is a mecca of lesbians, and I've enjoyed dating and sleeping with a variety of women. I'm not ashamed, but Hannah seems sheltered, and I worry about her reaction. Her judgment. If she's the kind of woman who wants to wait until marriage, she might also be the kind of woman who would find sleeping around scandalous. Or, perhaps worse, she might doubt my interest in her—if that's something that ever comes about. Not that it will, since she's getting married in less than a month.

These thoughts lead to another burning question I've had since the coffee shop. "How about your dating history?"

She wrinkles her nose, dunks a fry into her milkshake, and eats it in a series of small bites before answering. I recognize the delay tactic for what it is, and my curiosity skyrockets.

"There's really nothing to tell. I'm much too awkward to flirt, so the chance to date never really came up before. And now I'm engaged, so it won't come up again."

"Do you regret that?" *Stupid, stupid mouth.* I need to be quiet before I start asking questions about her potential interest in women.

"No." Hannah shakes her head firmly. "I definitely don't. I was never that interested in dating. Guys are just so…" She looks as though she's searching for the word. "I want to say *smelly*, but that would make me sound like an elementary schooler complaining about how boys have cooties."

I could faint. She thinks guys are smelly and was never really interested in dating them. *Maybe there's a chance*.

Shut up, Meli. Not liking smelly guys doesn't equate to liking *me*. When I crushed on Emma, she would often complain about her boyfriend, and every time I would get excited, wondering if that meant I had a chance with her. Of course, it never did. I shouldn't have to learn the same hard lesson again. I know better now.

I can be Hannah's friend. I can encourage her to see herself as the awesome person she is. But I just can't let myself believe I might have a chance with her.

"You look thoughtful." She points a new French fry at me. "Are you considering whether men really are smelly?"

"Oh, they are." I nod emphatically, wrinkling my nose to punctuate the gesture. "Why do you think I date women?"

Hannah laughs. "Fair enough. Have an onion ring." She holds one out to me and I take it. Our fingers brush.

"Thank you. I'm honored by this gift." I bow my head and she laughs again.

"You should be. Are you looking forward to my bachelorette party?"

"Definitely. It's on Friday, right?"

"Yep."

"And who planned it?"

"Eric's assistant, Lydia. She's in her early sixties, and Eric told her to keep things mellow, so I think we'll be drinking tea and doing some embroidery. It should be interesting."

"Sure, sure. Gotta love that tea. Will Crystal be there?" I'm hoping she was dismissed after the café fiasco, but something tells me that that isn't what happened.

Hannah sighs.

"Yes. I asked Eric if we could replace her, but everything is already too last minute and she's already signed a contract, so we're stuck with her. Plus," she leans forward, "I think he actually likes her for some reason."

"That is disturbing." Then I think I probably shouldn't insult Hannah's fiancé to her face. She is quiet for a moment.

"It is," she finally says. "Oh well. Everyone else seems nice. Tell me more about your friend Jen."

I go with her topic change.

We chat about the other bridesmaids while finishing the food, then Hannah suggests a walk. Before I realize it, it's almost ten p.m. and we've been strolling on the sidewalk by the river for several hours, just talking.

"I need to get home," Hannah moans. "I have work tomorrow."

"Same, although not until eleven. This was fun, though."

"Really?" Hannah seems a little surprised.

"Of course. You're fun to hang out with."

"Well, now that I'm actually able to talk to you, sure."

"That does help, but you were fun from the first meeting at the coffee shop." We stop less than a foot apart and face each other. Our hands rest inches away from each other on the railing. I don't want to go too far with my compliments and make Hannah uncomfortable, but she needs to realize how cool she is.

"So were you." Hannah grins, though she blushes, too. "But I'm sure everyone says that about you."

"Thanks." I tilt my head at her, a little confused by the comment. "What do you mean that everyone says that about me?"

"Because you're you." Hannah looks surprised that I even had to ask that question. "You're all…wonderful and stuff."

Wonderful and stuff. It's a hedgy compliment, but also one of the best I've ever received because it came from her.

"Thank you, Hannah. I think you're wonderful, too."

"Um, thanks." She blushes strawberry pink. Her humility

is adorably attractive, and I wonder what other colors she'd turn with more compliments. But as much as I'd like to continue this line of conversation, it's late, and she was just talking about work tomorrow.

"How are you getting home?"

"Probably the bus." She glances at her watch. "Definitely the bus. You?"

"Same." We compare timetables and discover we live close to each other. Or at least we will until she moves to Eric's apartment. Together, we take the bus toward home and continue a light banter until we wave good-bye at my stop. It is only when I'm walking home by myself that I notice my face is aching from smiling so big for so long.

Chapter Six

All right, dear." Lydia places her hand on mine. "How are you feeling?"

"I'm okay." I smile at her. Lydia has been Eric's assistant for years, and I've had a lot of interactions with her—mostly while trying to get in touch with Eric. She's a sweet woman who reminds me a little of a friendly older aunt. I guess that's why I usually don't struggle to speak with her. At least not much.

Lydia is at my apartment dropping off a box she says will come in handy during the party this evening. I've already sworn to her I will not open it before everyone arrives. My apartment is way too small for any kind of party, but I've spent a good amount of time scrubbing the floors and organizing my things, so I think it'll be tidy enough to not embarrass me. Or not too much. Or maybe it still will. I live in a studio, so my bed takes up most of one corner, the kitchen is little more than a nook, and the living room serves as a dining room, yoga studio, home office, and guest bedroom. If I ever were to have guests overnight. Which I will not.

"Well, I hope you'll enjoy your party."

"I'm sure I will, thanks so much for planning it."

"Of course, anything for you and Eric."

Lydia smiles and grabs her purple cat-print scarf and blue jacket from my coat peg on her way out. I walk her to the door, then flop onto the couch and look at the box with interest. I grin at the memory of the conversation Meli and I shared. Just as we imagined, the box is probably full of cakes or playing cards or tea, based on what I know about Lydia. I like all those things. This could be fun.

After a few pleasant moments of poking the box to see what's inside, I get up, stretch, and go for a quick run through the shower. As I step out, the doorbell rings and I freeze. When I planned how to handle this evening, I didn't consider what I might do if I were to be naked and wet when the doorbell rang. I throw my towel on and sidle to the door to peer through the peephole. Meli stands on the other side, hip jutting to one side. The tension in my chest unspools. I completely forgot we agreed she'd come an hour early to help set up—or at least, that I asked her to. I mostly just wanted to see Meli again. With Lydia handling all the party planning, there isn't a lot of set-up to do.

Tugging the towel closer, I undo the deadbolt and swing the door open.

"Hey Han—" Meli stares at me, and my face burns. I could have just asked her to wait outside while I put some clothes on. Of course, that idea didn't occur to me until just now, when it's too late. This is definitely a social interaction that I've handled poorly.

"Sorry!" My voice squeaks. I step out of the way to let her in and scamper toward the bathroom. "I'll just put s-some clothes on!" I don't even glance back to see if Meli has come in or closed the door behind her. I'm so embarrassed. Meli's going to think I'm incredibly strange for answering the door in a towel.

What if it's awkward when I go back out there?

It definitely will be.

Oh no.

In the bathroom, I quickly dry off, run a comb through my

hair, and pull on my underwear and bra. My dress is a white number with a short floaty skirt and a red belt that I loved in the shop when I tried it on. I step in and pull it past my thighs and hips, then slip my arms into the sleeves. I remember this going on a little more easily in the shop. Although, come to think of it, I also remember getting a little help with the zipper—

Oh no again. I can't zip the zipper. I reach one arm up and twist and wiggle, try to take it off again, and jump around a little. My arm just isn't long enough to reach the zip, no matter whether I stretch up or down. I've gotten myself into a terrible pickle. The whole back of my dress, from the top of my underwear up, is gaping open. And it's the only outfit I have in the bathroom with me. I might be able to make a dash to the bedroom, but Meli would see me running past half-naked—again.

"Meli?" I hear the hesitance in my voice. Silence. Maybe I made things so awkward she decided to stay in the hall. Finally, I hear her reply.

"Yes?"

I hold the dress up with one hand in the front while I tentatively slide open the bathroom door and pop my head around it. Meli sits on the couch, looking across the room toward the spice rack in my tiny kitchen with the air of someone fascinated by a beautiful painting. She doesn't turn at the sound of the bathroom door opening.

"Could you, um, please help me…with something?"

Now she does turn. I step out from around the door. I know without looking that I'm blushing as red as a tomato.

"I can't get my dress to zip. Could you…?"

"Of course. No problem. We've all been there, huh?" Meli walks to me, seeming to look everywhere except at me. I'm really not sure what's going on. Maybe she's embarrassed for me because of my snafu. Maybe it's because she's horrified at the thought of seeing me partially clothed again. Maybe that's just how friends are.

Maybe it's because Meli's a lesbian. That must be it. The realization almost knocks me over with relief. Meli isn't really horrified at the thought of seeing me half-naked, she's just trying not to make *me* uncomfortable. It's comforting to think that she's just worried about me. At least it isn't Kate all over again.

By now, Meli has made her way over to me, probably half by feel. I turn around to wait so I won't have to watch her trying to avoid looking at me. I'm still holding the front of the dress up with one hand. Little tingles travel up and down my spine, probably because of the slightly chilly air from the window I left cracked open. Probably.

Then Meli's hand brushes the small of my back.

"Mmm..."

I did not mean to make that sound. Meli jerks away.

"Sorry!" I turn quickly toward her. "It's, um, it's just cold in here. Please. I need your help." I flash her a smile to show her that I'm not uncomfortable, even though my legs feel a little like jelly. We change positions a third time, and there's the soft flutter of her touch again. One hand is warm and firm at my waist, while the other skims my back as she draws the zipper closed.

When Meli touches me, I feel shivery and warm, like nothing I've ever felt before. There's a strong draw to take a half step backward and into Meli's arms. I can't explain why that is, but my stomach knots at the realization.

"There you go." For a moment, Meli's fingertips skim along the top of my shoulder.

When I turn, Meli has stepped away and is looking with interest out the window. Part of me wants to grab her hand, just to feel her touch again.

But that's ridiculous. I'm about to marry Eric. There's no point in exploring why Meli's touch is so intoxicating.

"Thanks." I follow her into the living room, and we sit on

opposite ends of the couch. My discomfort is so intense I could keel over here and now, and based on the way Meli is tapping her fingers rhythmically against her leg, I think she's feeling awkward, too. I glance at my watch. There's still more than fifty minutes before the other guests arrive, and if we don't end this awkwardness soon, it's going to be a very long fifty minutes.

I should say something suave, maybe bring up a topic we both like. Like chocolate. Or being trees in plays. I try to focus on things that friends might talk about, but my thoughts keep drifting back to Meli's hands on my back. Under no circumstances should I suggest that she try touching me some more so that we could see what happens. That would be an unmitigated disaster, like when Ron tried to jinx Malfoy and instead turned the spell back on himself.

"Harry Potter!"

"What?" Meli seems confused, but a smile spreads across her face. Relief floods me. It worked! Meli may be confused, but at least neither of us is awkward or embarrassed now.

"I was just thinking…um…about how we both like Harry Potter."

"*That's* what you were thinking about?" Meli chuckles. "I was worried you would be creeped out by me seeing you in your bra."

"Why would I be?"

"Well, a lot of straight women might be a little uncomfortable being half-naked in front of a lesbian woman." Meli's voice is soft and low. "I just don't want you to feel that way."

"I don't." I want to reassure her. "I didn't…mind." I flush and look at my lap. "So, which of the Harry Potter books is your favorite? Or better yet, a ranking from one to seven." Meli may think I'm a complete weirdo for changing the subject like this, and I'll be the first to admit I'm not the most socially savvy, but if we keep talking about Meli zipping my dress, I'm worried I'll admit I liked the gentle skim of her fingers on my bare back.

We spend half an hour enthusiastically comparing our favorite Harry Potter scenes, then Meli helps set out the snacks I've prepared. There are cookies, chips and dip, carrot sticks, and popcorn. She sneaks a few pieces of popcorn and winks at me when I catch her. Things are back to normal between us—even though that wink brings me right back to the melting feeling I got in the café when she first winked at me.

The doorbell rings and Meli lets Jen in. Jen's wearing a black minidress, which looks very good on her but which I'd never wear in a million years. That thought turns my attention to Meli's outfit, which I hadn't noticed at first. She's wearing a pair of tight-fitting jeans and a white top that leaves her shoulders bare and crisscrosses her back with thin straps. My eyes are drawn back to those bare shoulders over and over, even as I try to distract myself by fiddling with the snacks and drinks.

I feel strange.

"Hey, Hannah, nice to see you again." Jen's smile is bright and genuine. "I love that dress."

"Thanks." I blush at the compliment and glance at Meli. I wonder if Meli's thinking about my dress, too. I wonder if she likes it. I wonder why it matters so much to me that she does.

Charlie arrives next, dressed casually but nicely in a pair of jeans and a fitted top. She's arranged her braids into one long braid down her back and has some intricate makeup on.

"Hey, Hannah." She nods at me as Jen lets her in. "Happy Bachelorette Party!"

"Thanks. Um, please have a seat."

Charlie joins us in the living room after grabbing a handful of snacks.

"I like your apartment," she says. "Your bedspread is great."

My bedspread is a boring dark blue, but I appreciate that Charlie has made the effort to compliment it anyway.

"Thank you." *I should probably ask her a question or make*

some comment back. As always, my mind blanks, but I still manage to land on a classic. "Um, how was your day?"

"Not bad." Charlie tosses her braid over her shoulder. "A little dull. We're in the middle of a big project and I honestly can't wait to escape to a Caribbean island for a week."

"Oh, same." Jen nods her agreement. "Work is a total drag right now. We have this really annoying client who seems to change what he wants every two seconds."

"I didn't know about that." Meli sounds a little surprised, but Jen just rolls her eyes.

"It isn't very interesting. Not like your job." Jen flips her hair over her shoulder, looking a little uncomfortable. "How's the play going?"

"Shin's doing an amazing job as director. He has this great vision and he's doing such a good job of explaining it to us. And there's this amazing scene where Ryan, who plays Hansel, and I are flying around on these wires…so cool." Meli glances to me. "How's your work?"

"It's okay." I'm hesitant to be drawn into the conversation since I enjoy talking more as a spectator sport, but it's Meli asking. I want to try. "I'm, um, writing some marketing copy about our new sandblaster, the Blast 3000. Every time I write about it, I feel like I'm talking about a water park. Or, um, a soft drink."

"*The Blast 3000.*" Meli makes her voice dramatic and low. "Fixes your walls and has a delicious lemon lime flavor." Her voice goes back to normal, and she frowns. "Do sandblasters fix your wall?"

"I mean, not by themselves?"

"Okay, okay." Her voice goes deep again. "*The Blast 3000.* Does something to your walls and has a delicious lemon lime flavor."

"Now also in grape," Jen adds.

For a few minutes, everyone makes fun of the Blast 3000

and I relax. I'm always going to be on edge in a group, but if I have to be part of one, this isn't so bad.

Finally, Crystal arrives almost ten minutes late. She wears a white dress, tall heels that she doesn't take off at the door like everyone else did, and way too much makeup for any occasion.

"Okay." Crystal stands at the edge of the living room and surveys us like we're her subjects. "Let's get this show on the road!"

All eyes turn to me, but this time, I'm ready. I practiced what I want to say. "So, this party was planned by Eric's assistant, um, Lydia. She dropped by this box of things she said we'd need, so we can start there." I gesture to the box.

Charlie smiles. Meli looks suitably impressed by my long and calm sentence. Even Jen gives me a thumbs-up. Only Crystal seems unimpressed.

"All right, then, open her up," she mumbles.

"Oh." Meli holds up a hand to stop us from diving into the box. "Before we start, Lydia is an elderly woman, and we should all be good sports about whatever is in the box."

I nod at Meli appreciatively, then reach forward and lift the lid off the box. My jaw drops. On top is a sparkly white crown that says *Bride-To-Be* along with about twenty sparkly clips to hold it in my hair. That's not the strangest part, though.

Almost everything in the box, apart from the crown, is shaped like the male sex organ. There are penis whistles, penis cookies in individual cellophane wrappers, and penis stickers.

"Uh, I thought you said this box was left by an *elderly* assistant of Eric's?" Jen raises her eyebrows. "This whole… vibe doesn't really fit."

Suddenly, all five of us, even Crystal, are laughing uproariously. This is just too funny. I'm trying to imagine Lydia, with her gray hair and her kind eyes, going to some party store and finding all these phallic-shaped party favors. I wonder if

Lydia knew what she was doing, or if this was all some kind of online shopping mix-up. I'm not sure which would be funnier.

Apparently, I'm not the only one with questions, because Charlie's voice is a little high from laughing so long and loud. "Maybe she just ordered a whole prepackaged bachelorette kit online."

"That could be it." Meli nods. "Or maybe Lydia is just, uh, sexually progressive?"

"I guess we'll never know." Jen shakes her head with mock solemnity.

"Come on, girls!" We turn to Crystal, who has already stuck several penis stickers on her face. "What are you waiting for?"

We are all laughing again. I worried this bachelorette party was going to be tense, but the box of penises lightened the mood. I should keep that in mind for future gatherings.

"I love this crown." Crystal has dug back into the box and grabbed the plastic *Bride-To-Be* crown. It's tacky and hideous, in my opinion, but there's no accounting for taste.

"You can have it." I give her a thumbs-up and Crystal places it on her head.

"Are you sure?" Charlie looks back and forth between me and Crystal, her brow crinkling.

"It's really fine." I reach into the box and pull out a deck of bachelorette-themed playing cards. "I'm more interested in this."

We continue to ransack the box and giggle uncontrollably as we show each other our finds. Just as we've settled down a little, the doorbell rings.

"Are we missing someone?" Meli asks.

"I bet it's Eric!" Crystal shrieks at the exact same moment.

I can't help but wonder if she knows that Eric is the man *I'm* scheduled to marry next week, given her completely unabashed flirting, but I can't bring myself to care much.

"Do you want to get the door?" Meli asks.

I shake my head. I hate answering the door, especially if I don't know who's going to be there. I'm always worried it might be someone who wants to sell me something and I'll end up with, like, a full set of encyclopedias or a fancy kitchen gadget I don't want.

"Wimp," Crystal mutters. She flounces to the door, her white skirts swinging around her long legs. Outside is a policeman—or at least someone who looks a lot like a policeman. My heart sinks. Lydia did *not* hire a male stripper. That seems a step too far.

On the other hand, Lydia did drop off a box of penises.

"We have a noise complaint from next door." The man's voice is deep and serious. Maybe he really is a policeman and I'm about to get fined for all the laughing.

"Oh no, I'm *so sorry*, Officer." Crystal's voice is high-pitched and fluttery.

"I'm afraid I'll have to discipline you," the stripper continues. He's definitely a stripper, because no real police officer would say something so provocative. He looks Crystal up and down and probably assumes she's the bride given her white dress, penis facial stickers, and crown. His hips undulate as he leads her into the living room and sits her on a kitchen chair. He turns on a portable speaker. Then, with music blaring, he starts gyrating at her.

I'm laughing so hard I can barely breathe. Beside me, Meli is in stitches, too. I thought strippers were meant to be sexy, but maybe he was hired as a comedian. There's nothing attractive about a man in tearaway pants as far as I'm concerned.

"Do you want me to correct him?" Meli asks me between fits of giggles. "I could let him know that you're the bride." Crystal is lounging on the kitchen chair, nodding her head to the music, and seemingly in no hurry to let him know that she isn't, in fact, about to be married. Since she seems perfectly comfortable, I see no reason to interject.

"Please don't." I am breathless. "That looks terrible. I do not want to be involved." Crystal starts sliding singles into the man's waistband. She must have been prepared for this, or at least brought her wallet with her. No matter, I'd sooner crawl into a hole than take her place. I'm much happier here, bent into stitches, holding Meli's hand.

Holding Meli's hand.

It's true. Sometime in the middle of our laughter, we laced our fingers together. I don't want to let go.

And that's when it hits me like a stale pretzel dropped by a passing seagull—which really happened to me once while my family was living in Florida. I understand now why I'm always so excited to see Meli. Why I shivered when she touched me. Why I desperately want to hold her hand.

I have a crush on Meli.

Oh no.

CHAPTER SEVEN

Saint Sofia, here we come!"

Jen is way, way, way too enthusiastic for four in the morning. She came over to my apartment last night—allegedly to sleep. Instead of sleeping, though, we watched sitcoms and ate popcorn until just a few hours ago. Now I wish we'd just met at the airport, because it is way too early and I'm in no mood.

I tell myself I'm grumpy because it's basically the middle of the night. Of course, it's more complicated than that. It's been a week since Hannah's bachelorette party and a week since she's spoken to me. She replied to a few texts, but just to say she was busy.

The dress-zipping must have freaked her out more than she let on.

It certainly freaked me out. She'd been wearing a lacy white bra and my hand had stilled for just a heartbeat over the clasp. Worse had been the matching underwear just visible at the end of the zipper. And worse than any of that, Hannah isn't even talking to me now.

Well, I will see her today as the week of wedding festivities begins on Saint Sofia. At the end of the day, I'm getting paid to travel to a tropical island and participate in said festivities. I'm getting paid to zipline and swim with dolphins and attend networking dinners. Those activities were on the laminated agenda couriered to me a few days ago, along with helpful suggestions on what to wear. The agenda also mentioned that there would be ample meeting time, presumably for Eric to make his business connections, and noted that he would be the MC of many of the activities. He's the real star of the weekend.

Oh, and I'm getting paid to serve as Hannah's maid of honor. That bit of news was also included in the couriered package. She's not speaking to me, and I get a front row seat to an event I'd rather not even see happen—and an active role in the festivities.

"Saint Sofia, here we come." I echo Jen, but with much, much less enthusiasm. She shares a bracing smile.

"It's going to be okay." She gently grips my shoulder. "You don't always get the girl, but we always have a good time."

"I'm not trying to *get* Hannah," I lie blatantly. "I'm just trying to get her to understand she deserves better. Though it's probably too late."

"But we do still get to swim with dolphins and zipline and eat chicken, fish, or vegetables."

I sigh. Jen is a great friend. I should stop sulking.

"And wear pretty dresses," I add. I've always enjoyed a good costume to fit my role, although I'm a little concerned about the bridesmaid dress I got measured for last week.

"That's more like it! Now, let's gooooo!"

Jen leads the charge out of the apartment and down the stairs, where we drag our suitcases three blocks to the bus station, catch the bus to the MAX station, and ride the MAX to the airport. Oh, the glamorous life of people who don't own a car and can't afford a taxi. We're traveling with the night crew of Portland, a mix of people working late shifts at hospitals, airports, and bars, and people who don't have a home to go to and would rather be warm on a bus than cold in the rain. As we get closer to the airport, I spot someone who might be Charlie, but she's got her earbuds in and falls into the flood of people exiting the MAX before I can say hello.

By the time we arrive at the airport, even Jen looks a bit worn around the edges. We check in and shuffle through security, which is relatively empty at this time of night. On my suggestion, we go straight to the gate, where Jen collapses into a chair while I lean against the window. I want to savor every moment of verticality I can before I have to sit for the next six hours.

"Will the rest of the bridesmaids be here?" Jen asks.

"I think so. Eric said the boat to Saint Sofia leaves from Saint Mary at three in the afternoon sharp and that we shouldn't miss it. So probably everyone is on this flight. And I think I saw Charlie on the bus."

"I wish we could have taken the private jet," Jen grumbles. I sigh. The thought of Eric and Hannah on his jet is a bit more than I want to deal with at this time of the night. I can imagine the one-sided conversation—Eric telling Hannah she has to be friendly at the wedding and Hannah nodding along, miserable and guilty.

"Hey."

I turn toward the softest of voices. *Hannah is here*.

I do a double take to make sure it's really her, here in the airport in the early morning. It is. She wears a pair of gray sweatpants and a pink top with *Sprinkles* across the chest. Her hair is piled into a messy bun on top of her head. She looks tired but happy.

"Hannah!" It's awkward to just stand in front of her, so I pull her into a quick hug. She still smells like cinnamon. I let go before I can notice anything else—like how good she feels in my arms. "What are you doing here?"

"Eric and I agreed it would be best to meet there." She glances around to make sure no one is listening, then she leans a little closer. “He wanted to fly with a bunch of his businessman friends, and he asked if I was going to be social, and I said no, and he said I should just fly commercial, then.” She grins. “I think he thinks it’s a punishment, but I’m just as happy to not have to pretend to be fancy with all of his stuck-up business partners.”

I have a lot of thoughts on that.

“His loss, our gain.”

Hannah’s grin widens. She looks way too enthusiastic for this time of the morning, but it’s catching. All my worry about her not reaching out slips away in her presence. She’s herself. Maybe she really was just busy all week.

“I’m going to buy a hot drink for the flight,” she says. “Would you like to come with?”

“Sure!” Now *I* sound way too enthusiastic for this time of the morning. “Jen—”

“Of course I’ll watch the bags.” Jen agrees without me even asking the question. She flops her hand in a clear dismissal, still looking at her phone. “Get me a red-eye or something. I want to be full of energy for my tropical getaway.”

“If you drink one now, you’ll just be full of energy for the long flight.” Jen just shrugs. “Okay, fine, be hyper, then. Shall we, Hannah?”

We drop our backpacks on the seats next to Jen and head toward the small café in the center of the concourse. We join the short line and crane our necks to read the menu.

“Cherry blossom frappé,” Hannah reads. She turns to me. “Do you think that’s to celebrate springtime?”

“I would assume so, especially since there’s an Easter egg mocha right next to it.”

“Do you think it’s terrible?”

“Probably.”

“I’m going to get one.” She visibly bounces. “Maybe the cherry blossom hot chocolate.”

I give her a little side-eye.

"You seem cheerful."

Suddenly, the bouncing stops, and she turns to me. Her excitement at reading out the drink names has disappeared.

"I'm actually terrified."

"Really?"

She nods.

"I know that Eric is the guy for me. I mean, he has to be. And this wedding is what my parents have always wanted. But the idea of being married to him is terrifying. I know I just need to come out of my shell more, but the idea of having to talk to a bunch of people every day for the rest of my life is just as scary. And I know that's what he expects of me. He wants me to join him at all his social events and be friendly and…"

"Hannah." I grab her hand and pull her out of the line, even though we were almost at the front. She follows me around the corner and into an abandoned gate full of empty seats and one snoozing gentleman. I walk us to the backside of the check-in desk before I speak. We can see the early morning clouds and the flash of aircraft lights out the window overlooking the landing strips. "I know I sound like a broken record, but there's nothing wrong with you not wanting to talk to people. If being more talkative is one of your goals, that's great, but you shouldn't have to force yourself to change because of someone else."

"I know." She pauses. "There's one thing I've been thinking about a lot." She bites her lip. The gesture is so unbelievably sexy I'm pretty sure I'm about to start drooling. "This is going to sound a little strange."

"Try me."

"Well…" Hannah hesitates. "I, um…well, I haven't kissed a lot of people."

Oh God. I'm not sure this can go anywhere good. She seems to be waiting for me to say something.

"How many is not many?" This isn't really something I

need to know, but it's better to say something than just to stare at her.

"Eric and two others. But one of them was when we were both really young."

"Okay."

We stand there for a minute. There are just a few inches separating us. Hannah's back is against the wall. I should move away.

I don't.

"So, when I kiss Eric, I don't…feel that much. And I'm wondering if I should feel more."

A wave of hope and attraction floods me, but I hold myself back.

"Okay."

"When you, um, kiss someone you like, do…you, um…do you feel a lot?"

This is surreal. First, Hannah doesn't talk to me for nearly a week. Then she shows up in the airport and asks me about kissing at five o'clock in the morning. If I didn't know better, I'd think she was messing with me. But I do know better. Hannah is doing her very best to tell me something that's hard for her to say.

"Yes." My thoughts are only seconds ahead of my words, so I speak slowly. "It feels nice. I mean, some people talk about fireworks, and I wouldn't necessarily say I feel that, but it's nice. It feels *right*. With the right person, it's exciting, comforting, and just, uh, good. Did you feel anything like that with your other kisses?"

"I don't know." Hannah's voice is soft and low, and I lean closer in. She's pulling me in, just with her words. I think she's closer, too. Her lips are slightly parted, and her eyes are wide. "I wondered if—"

"There you are!"

We whirl around like kids caught with one hand in the

cookie jar to find Crystal, hands on her hips. Unlike our travel comfy-casual garb, she's dressed in stilettos and a miniskirt with her face completely made up and her hair curled. Maybe she thought Eric would be on the flight.

"Good morning, Crystal," I say resignedly.

"We were looking for you," she huffs. "Boarding is starting."

"Thanks for the heads-up." I fake smile at her, and she returns the gesture before flouncing back toward our gate. Her butt sways visibly beneath her skirt and I look away.

"What were you saying?" I turn back to Hannah, but she's already closed back up like a turtle slipping back into its shell.

"Nothing." Her smile is stiff, and it doesn't quite reach her eyes. "I was being silly. I wanted to apologize for ghosting you this week. It's just been ridiculously busy with wedding preparations."

I'm suspicious, but it's clear she's done with our conversation, and I don't want to push. Even if I'm half-sure she planned to kiss me.

"Don't worry, I assumed you just had a lot of wedding-related tasks to do. Shall we head back?" As we emerge into the bright lights and bustle of the rest of the terminal, I second-guess myself. I just misread that situation. The odds Hannah was planning to kiss me are infinitesimal, no matter how much she bit her lip and asked about kissing. She's just…inexperienced. She probably didn't know what she was doing. It isn't her fault I wanted nothing more than to pull her into my arms and kiss her breathless.

"Where's my red-eye?" Jen asks when we get back to our gate.

"Uh, that didn't happen."

Jen sighs. "Of course. Well, when I'm fast asleep on the beach while everyone else is befriending dolphins, I'll know exactly who to blame."

"It was my fault." I turn to Hannah in surprise. It's the first time I've heard her purposefully join a conversation that wasn't with me. "I had to apologize to Meli for ignoring her this week."

"Hmm." I hear Jen's suspicion. "*Anyway*, I'm going to go join the boarding line and shuffle along dismally with my fellow Caribbean travelers." With that, she gets to her feet, swings her backpack onto her slim shoulders, and heads off to join the line. Hannah and I quickly grab our bags and follow, trading amused looks.

For the moment, the strangeness of the almost-kiss seems forgotten. It's a little like when a scene ends and I run backstage, coming back to who I really am piece by piece as the intensity of being onstage fades away. I'm more certain than ever that Hannah was not trying to kiss me.

Yet part of me still clings to how she looked, standing in front of me, biting her lip, her eyes so wide, and so full of hope.

Chapter Eight

I'm so mad at myself. As I sink into my first-class seat, which Eric insisted on buying for me so I wouldn't be with everyone else, my heart clenches. I can't believe that just happened. Almost happened. Again. I almost kissed a girl. Again. I thought I was over having feelings for other girls, even though a part of me had always known the attraction I felt all those years ago could come back.

"Have a nice flight!" Meli waves to me. I wave back as she continues down the aisle to her seat in the main cabin. I wish she was sitting next to me, but I'm also glad she's not. Charlie passes a minute later, smiling a polite good morning to me. I smile back and lift my hand in a wave.

I was being ridiculous anyway, off in a dark corner with Meli. I thought of her all week. A fuzzy plan formed in my head to kiss her. Just once. I just had to know if the shivers I experienced when she touched me would intensify with a kiss. And I almost ruined everything. I don't know what Eric would do if he found out I kissed someone else—and a woman at that—on the way to our wedding.

And worse, Meli…

It was very likely Meli wouldn't have wanted to kiss me back. She's amazing, interesting, full of life. I'm quiet and shy and plain, nothing like Meli, with her gorgeous dark eyes and hair. And even if Meli *did* want me, being with her would mean sacrificing my family, my marriage, and my future. I've let my parents down a million times before with my shyness and my awkwardness. I can't let them down again. Even if I still wonder how it would feel to kiss Meli.

Perhaps the worst of all is that I've been here before.

Kate was my best friend. We were only eleven, but we stood at the center of a group of giggling girls, always on the phone with each other, always sleeping over at each other's houses. We started ballet classes together and helped each other make neat buns before class. Even better, my family lived next door to hers in Colorado Springs for almost a year, longer than we'd lived anywhere in a long time. I was shy then, too, but Kate drew me out, made me feel special and seen. With her around, I felt…almost confident.

Then, one night, I slept over at her house. Kate started dreaming aloud about our friendship, how we'd rule high school, then go to college together and be roommates when we worked in New York City. We'd raise our kids together.

Drunk on her words, I leaned forward and planted a quick, glancing kiss on her cheek.

There was a long pause, then Kate freaked out. She rolled from the bed we were sharing and ran to her parents' room, crying.

After hearing Kate's story, her parents drove me home while I sobbed in the back seat. I didn't know her family was very religious and taught her since infancy that being gay was a sin. I'd been told that my whole life, too, but I'd been so caught up in the moment that I'd been willing to forget everything.

My parents grounded me for a month for inappropriate behavior when Kate's parents told them what had happened. If I'd been a little older or had kissed Kate on the mouth instead of the cheek, they might well have sent me to conversion camp.

Even worse was what happened at school. Kate told everyone that I'd attacked her in the night and tried to kiss her. She said that I might have been taken over by the devil. I knew what really happened, but I wasn't able to speak up for myself to set the record straight. After that, no one would talk to me. No one would dance next to me in ballet.

Two months later, my dad was reassigned to a post in Texas. My parents forgot what had happened with Kate, or at least they never brought it up again. And I gave up, once and for all, on making friends and on listening to my heart. It brought nothing but disaster.

Now, once again, idiot that I am, I'd been ready to throw it all away. After a week of being smart, of steering well clear of Meli after I realized my feelings go way beyond friendship, all it took was one conversation for me to want to leap into her arms like a Disney princess.

"Are you all right, dear?"

I startle from my thoughts to realize that the elderly gentleman next to me has looked up from his magazine to fix me with a concerned stare.

"Mm-hmm." I smile but rummage through my backpack for my book, or anything else I can use to keep from engaging in conversation with this man. I just don't think I can handle talking right now. I secure my book and a pair of headphones, but he still looks at me. *Oh no*. I must really be a mess.

"Would you like a chocolate?" The man now produces an enormous heart-shaped box of chocolates from somewhere in his carry-on and extends it to me across the wide armrest that separates our seats. Something about the sight is amusing and endearing enough to bring a smile to my face, and I take one.

"Thank you." I bite into the chocolate, and caramel explodes in my mouth. *Delicious.*

"You seem sad."

I mumble and point apologetically to my full mouth, but he's undeterred.

"Don't be sad, dear. We're on our way to a tropical paradise!"

I nod.

"It's my first time traveling since my wife died," he continues. The man selects a chocolate for himself. "And even *I'm* not sad. Well, of course, I'm sad, but I'm happy, too. She planned this whole trip for me before she died because she wanted me to get out and enjoy life for the both of us."

"I'm, um, so sorry about your wife." Finally, the right words come to me at the right time. Thank goodness.

"Me too. But we had almost fifty years together. A love like that doesn't come around every day." He winks and extends the box of chocolates again. I take another. Then, humming to himself, he pokes experimentally at his video screen.

I bite the chocolate in half with a little more force than necessary and chomp the raspberry and cream filling. If this man can be happy after having lost his wife of fifty years, I can be happy on the way to my own wedding. I just need to forget all my doubts and get on board with getting married. Sure, I don't have the same deep flame of attraction with Eric I do with Meli, but that will come with time. It has to. And even if it doesn't, Eric and I can be partners. It's all fine.

Yet I spend the remaining hours of the flight listening to my favorite playlist, gazing at the sunrise out the window, and imagining what it might be like to slide my hands into Meli's wonderful hair and pull her close. I can picture what it would be like to kiss her, and I can feel how soft her lips would be, but my imagination fails me after that.

By the time we land in Saint Mary, I'm in a strange mood. I am jumpy and raw from emotion, plus, as soon as we step out of the plane into the warm tropical air, I realize I'm overdressed in my sweatpants. I wait for Meli and Jen on the tarmac at the bottom of the stairs, though Crystal is the first one off from the main cabin.

Now her short skirt seems much more appropriate. She appraises me with some distaste per her usual. Her gaze lingers on my sweatpants.

"I see you decided not to change on the plane." Her tone is condescending. If I were a different person, a forthright person like Meli, I would tell her that I see that she decided not to change her personality, which is a shame. She would slink away. Unfortunately, I'm only that kind of person in my own head. So I just shrug. She tosses her hair over her shoulder and moves on.

Minutes later, Meli and Jen emerge with their arms linked and in deep conversation. I immediately feel I shouldn't disturb them. Before they catch sight of me, I fall into the crowd and let myself be swept into the airport.

"Hannah!"

Apparently, I wasn't fast enough. I turn around and wave at Jen.

"How was your flight?" Meli asks. She and Jen drop their arms and come to stand on either side of me. Then, suddenly, Jen's linking her arm through mine like she was doing with Meli, and Meli's doing the same on my other side. It's…strange, but nice.

"It was okay." That's an overstatement, to say the least. Almost the whole flight I was like a moody teenager who couldn't get a hold of her feelings. "How about yours?"

"Jen fell asleep," Meli says conspiratorially. "Like, as soon as we started taxiing."

"Because you didn't get me coffee!" Jen leans around me to shoot Meli a pointed look.

"Yes, because you would really have benefited from being awake for that flight." Meli rolls her eyes and exchanges a friendly glance with me. "Meanwhile, I couldn't sleep a wink."

"What were you doing, then?"

"Mostly just listening to music and watching the sky." Meli shrugs.

My heart practically skips a beat at the thought of Meli a few rows back doing the same thing I was. Maybe she was thinking of me while I was thinking of her.

Of course, she probably wasn't. Just because I've figured out why I'm having romantic feelings for Meli doesn't mean she's suddenly begun to feel the same way. I need to treat her the same way I always have, the same way she's always treated me—as a friend.

We enter the airport, all relaxing at the rush of cold air, and head through customs. Charlie is a few zags of the line behind us, reading a paperback book. The customs process is pretty quick and painless, especially since we aren't staying in Saint Mary, and it isn't long before we're out in the lobby. A man in a flower-covered T-shirt holds a large sign that reads *Hannah's Wedding.* A small crowd is already standing around him.

"Hi, Mom. Hi, Dad." My parents turn, and their faces break into huge smiles. My mom is wearing her usual long skirt and top and my dad is in a button-up, looking ready to walk into my wedding ceremony right now.

"Hannah!" They step forward, taking turns to hug me. "How was the flight?"

"Good, um, and yours? I guess it was a long way from North Dakota?" My parents are currently at a base there, which my dad says will be his last, but no one believes him. He could no sooner retire from military life than I could become a stand-up comedian.

"Not bad." My dad beams. "Anything for my little girl. My little girl who's about to get married!"

"We weren't sure this day would come for you," my mom adds. My dad nods.

"What with your thing about talking to people," he says,

"we worried no one would be patient enough to get to know you!"

I nod, but my heart squeezes. My parents are so proud I'm getting married, just like they always wanted. I can't let them down.

"Is Brad here already?" I look around and spot him shaking hands with Jen. My throat constricts. I was too embarrassed to tell my family about my fake bridesmaids, and I'm not sure how they'll introduce themselves or how they'll react.

"Brad!" My father uses his no-nonsense commander tone. "Come say hello to your sister."

Brad smiles at Jen, then strides over to envelop me in a bone-crushing hug. Brad is three years older than me and almost my exact opposite. He's confident, flirty, funny, and he makes his living through a surfboarding school in California. My parents were suspicious at first, but when the business took off, they embraced him as an entrepreneur.

"How's my little nugget?" My brother musses my hair with one hand like I'm still ten years old. Instead of being annoying, it feels familiar.

"Good." I smile. He's tanned, though I can still make out the freckles he has had since he was a little boy. And he's still much taller than me, just like he always has been.

"How are you feeling about the wedding?"

I shrug. I know how I feel, and I'm comfortable talking to Brad, but I'm not interested in putting my feelings into words. I'm not even sure how I would.

"How's the surf school?" I ask instead.

"Totally rad, bro." Brad makes an exaggerated hang ten sign and nudges me with his shoulder. "How's Portland?"

"Totally rad," I mock him. He rolls his eyes at me, then leans in conspiratorially.

"I met Jen." He looks back at her over his shoulder. "What's her story?"

Here we go.

"Her story?" I smirk at him. I know what he means, but I'm not making it easy for him. He's barely spoken to me.

"Yeah. Is she single?"

I burst out laughing. Of course, Brad is more worried about Jen's relationship status than anything else. Brad can be a bit of a player with pretty women, and I wouldn't be surprised if he spends most of my wedding on the lookout for potential love interests for himself. That's fine with me. The fewer eyes on me, the happier I am. If his exploits draw attention away from the wedding, that would be a good thing.

"I'm not sure." I'm still smiling as I shrug.

"Don't worry." Brad tips an imaginary cap to me and winks. "I'll find out."

"Best of luck to you. Not that you need it." I wink back. Although we don't talk very often now that we're both adults with our own lives, my brother remains one of the few people with whom I don't struggle to speak. I'm glad that ease hasn't faded with time. Brad hurries back toward Jen and I scan the crowd.

I wonder where Meli is.

As if on cue, she appears next to me.

"Hey." I smile. "These are my parents, Jana and Chad Barnes. Mom, Dad, this is Meli."

"Hello, Mr. and Mrs. Barnes." Meli extends her hand for a friendly shake and smiles politely. "It's lovely to meet you."

"Oh, please, call me Jana." My mother's words are kind, but she looks uncomfortable. "It's nice to meet you, Meli. Are you a friend of Hannah's?"

"I am." Meli smiles and links her arm with me. It seems like she really does think of me as a friend by now, even though that's not how things started out.

"Oh, good." My father shakes his head and leans in

conspiratorially. "We worried Hannah would never make friends. She's so—"

"Shy," my mother supplies helpfully. I want to sink into a hole and die, but Meli seems unfazed. She slings her arm across my shoulders in a way I'm sure is normal and friendly and pulls me against her side.

"What an...*interesting* thing to say." Meli dimples, but her smile doesn't match her eyes. Her eyes are steely. She's standing up for me, which makes me stand a little straighter.

"I think we'd better get moving." I end the conversation quietly. "The man with the sign looks like he's trying to herd people out."

"Well." My mother picks up her bag and turns to my father. "Let's go." She flashes a smile at me and somehow disappears into the small group. I sigh at the terrible sense of déjà vu. My parents left me alone in the middle of hundreds of social situations to fend for myself. They told me it was the only way I would gain more confidence.

Instead, I would panic and leave or just retreat even further into the background.

Now I'm an adult and I can handle myself, so I try not to let their disappearance bother me. Plus, I have Meli.

"Chad and Jana." Meli watches my parents stride out the door with something akin to horrified fascination.

"Sorry." I wrinkle my nose. "They're really friendly, but they're also quite focused on how shy I am."

"Right. Because when it's just us, you're sooooo shy. Maybe, instead of making you feel bad, they could think of ways to help you be a little more comfortable speaking in public." Meli wiggles her eyebrows playfully. "Anyway, off to paradise."

She takes her arm back and my shoulders are suddenly cool despite the warmth of the tropics. I cover my disappointment that she isn't touching me anymore by grabbing my backpack and swinging it onto one shoulder. Then I lead the way toward the doors.

"Are you looking forward to the festivities?"

"Sure, some of them. I've heard about the dolphin swim and some other things, like ziplining, which sound great. But there also seem to be a lot of fancy dinners…and I just don't feel like myself at those things."

"Me neither!" I shake my head. "I used the wrong fork at a dinner the other week and Eric got so huffy I thought he was going to pass out."

"You deserve better." Meli immediately covers her mouth like she wants to take the words back. "Sorry. I shouldn't have said that."

"You think I deserve better?" We're almost at the van that will take us to the harbor and the ferry, but I stop on the sidewalk and turn to her. "I think I'm *lucky* Eric is willing to put up with me."

"If you feel like you're just being tolerated, that's another sign you deserve better." Meli shrugs like her opinion and this conversation don't matter, but her brown eyes are unusually intense. She's looking straight into my soul. "I'm not saying you shouldn't marry him. I'm just saying you should take the time you still have to consider if marrying him is what you really want."

"I…" For the first time in a while, I'm speechless in front of Meli. She takes a deep breath, and softly exhales.

"I'm really sorry. I know that was over the line. I'll give you some space, okay?" She turns away to climb into the van. I stand rooted in the same spot for another minute before I follow her, wishing she'd given me another minute to get my thoughts together. I copy her deep inhale and long sigh. Another minute wouldn't have helped. I'm not sure what I would have said.

The idea of *better* lodges in the back of my mind like a popcorn kernel and won't get out. I'm not sure exactly what *better than Eric* means, but the image that pops into my mind is Meli, holding my hand, winking at me. If that isn't better, I don't know what is.

CHAPTER NINE

The whole drive to the pier and the whole ride on the ferry (which it seems like Eric has hired out for his wedding), what I said to Hannah repeats in my mind. Yes, I think Hannah deserves better, but I'm not usually so reckless and impulsive. I probably ruined everything with her. I doubt we'll even be friends now. I can't come back from insulting her fiancé, no matter how much of a jerk he really is.

Hannah spends the whole trip in conversation with her brother. There's an easy comradery there that warms my heart, especially after how stilted Hannah was around her parents. It seems like she has hardly any affirming people in her life.

Jen, meanwhile, leans against the railing next to me, keeping up a steady stream of chatter. She doesn't seem to notice I'm deep in a personal crisis.

"Is that the island?" She's literally bouncing on her toes. I crane my neck forward.

I'm momentarily distracted from my thoughts about Hannah as we watch Saint Sofia rise from the blue ocean. "I think you're right." It really is a tropical paradise. The island is small and lushly green, with white-sand beaches and a few beautifully designed buildings with sweeping windows. There are a few private boats at a large pier directly ahead and a small collection of airplanes on a landing strip on the far side. High on one hill is something that looks like a helicopter. There are several pools in front of the resort, as well as a second pier from which people dive into the pristine water below.

"Wow." Jen shakes her head, then throws an arm around my shoulder and squeezes. "I know I was suspicious about this whole fake bridesmaid thing, but thank you a million times for the *Buddy-Up* call." She pauses and assumes an exaggerated thinking position. "Should I become an actor? I could get used to this."

"It is not usually this glamorous." I wink.

"What are we going to do first?" She's practically vibrating from excitement. "I want to swim. I have my swimsuit on. Do you?"

"No." I pull away to shoot Jen a distressed look. "When did you put a swimsuit on?"

"In Portland! I just couldn't wait."

"So, you've been wearing a swimsuit all day."

"Yep!" Jen laughs.

"I am scandalized. And a little grossed out."

"Come on, it's a bikini, so it's not really that different from a bra and underwear."

"Wait—is it that thong bikini?"

"Sure is." Jen winks. She bought a very revealing red thong bikini on a shopping trip about a year ago and constantly threatens to wear it, even though it's little more than a few triangles of cloth on pieces of dental floss. "Why aren't you wearing yours?"

"Because I'm a *normal* person," I say. "I'll go to our room and change in two minutes. Like a *normal person*."

On the other side of the boat, Hannah laughs. I busy myself trying not to wish I was the one making her laugh.

"Stop it," Jen says gently. She traces my gaze to Hannah. "You told her she deserves better than her fiancé. That crosses a line, sweetie. You have to give her space."

"I know."

"And she's straight, anyway. And even if she weren't, she's engaged! Don't let this ruin our trip, okay?"

"I know." I fold my arms and glare at the approaching island. Jen is right, as usual, but that doesn't mean I don't resent her for it. I know I need to give Hannah space. I just don't want to.

"Sorry." Jen's mouth turns down and she flicks her hair over her shoulder. It's a tell that she's uncomfortable. "Hannah really does seem great."

"Yeah."

"Let's talk about something else. I read on the agenda that tonight's dinner is a seafood extravaganza. What do you think that is?"

"Something Hannah won't like." I can't help myself from throwing the comment out there, even though I know I should let my thoughts of Hannah go.

"Ugh!" Jen playfully swats my arm. "Come on, girl. *You* like fish. Focus on that!"

"I know, I know. Sorry. I do love fish. What's the dessert?"

"Chocolate lava cake." Jen seems to accept my apology, because she launches into a dissection of the menu over the next couple of days. I do my best to follow along.

A few minutes later the boat gently bumps into the dock and the crowd begins to disembark. Jen grabs my hand and tries to push to the very front of the crowd, although I don't think there's much point. We are barely on the dock before we're caught in a bottleneck. Eric has walked from behind a building and now stands on the dock with a bundle of flowers in his arms while a string quartet plays a romantic number behind him.

"This must be the real reason why he didn't want Hannah to fly with him," Jen says. She glances at me, then shakes her head. "Come on, even you have to admit this is romantic."

"Is it?" I wrinkle my nose, but I can't look away from the

sight of Eric with his arms full of flowers. Maybe this is the kind of romance that sells blockbuster movies and warms hearts, but I wonder how Hannah will receive the gesture. I think she'll hate being the center of attention. But maybe I'm wrong. We don't really know each other all that well.

As I predicted, Hannah emerges onto the dock, looking as far as I can imagine from a woman being swept off her feet. Everyone melts to the side to let her up to the front and she approaches Eric with her hands clasped together. The two of them are on display, almost on stage, and I can sense Hannah's nerves from where I stand. Eric looks her up and down, taking in the sweatpants, the Sprinkles top, and the messy bun. His mouth curls down slightly. He does not seem pleased. Probably the pictures of relaxed-outfit Hannah that the photographer is currently snapping aren't the ones he had in mind for this little performance. *What a jerk.* He really expected her to show up in a pretty dress and makeup after hours of flying so that he could put on a show. Even though I put on shows for a living, I would never do that to another person.

Still, Eric leans in for a kiss and sets the flowers in her arms as though he's handing over a baby. Hannah accepts them and takes a sniff. Her back is to me now, so I can't see her expression.

Eric pulls her in for a few more posed shots. The crowd is cooing, but I've seen enough. I take Jen's arm and lead us around the couple and toward the hotel. I allow myself one glance back at the two of them. They have their arms around each other, and Hannah's face is half-hidden behind flowers.

"Let's get checked in and then into the water."

Jen squeezes my arm. "I'm so in."

The receptionist directs us to a forest-view room on the ground floor. Thanking her, we take the keys and head in the direction of our home for the week. Jen lets us in.

"Well, this is…cozy." She flicks on the light. I giggle.

We're in a postage-stamp sized room with a tiny window that looks out onto a bush and a maintenance road.

"Do you think Eric doesn't like us, or does his hotel just suck?" Jen rubs her chin.

"Maybe both. Or he just doesn't want to spend too much money on our accommodations after paying us to be bridesmaids in the first place."

"Could be." I toss my bag onto the bed closer to the door, zip it open, and grab my swimsuit from where I tossed it last night in a frenzy of last-minute packing. "It hardly matters, anyway. I imagine we're going to be in the water most of the time."

"I hope you're planning to find another place to shower afterward," Jen peeks into the bathroom, "because I'm not sure I can fit a whole leg in this shower, much less all of me."

She's not being that dramatic. The shower is miniscule. I squeeze in experimentally and I fit, though I don't have room to turn around. That's going to make for some pretty exciting showers. I might have to turn off the water and get out of the shower for a new wash angle.

"Are you changed yet?" Jen asks impatiently.

"Almost!" I peel myself out of the shower and quickly change into my one-piece, banging my elbow on the strangely tall sink as I do so. It seems like a weird design choice to build a sink that reaches to the bottom of one's ribs, but I'm no designer. Outside, Jen's already stripped to her teeny bikini and is admiring herself in the full-length, yet oddly distorted, mirror.

"That took *forever*," she says theatrically. I roll my eyes. "Way more than two minutes. Come on! We only have a week on this island, and we better make the most of it!"

I shift, a little uncomfortable in my suit next to gorgeous Jen, but before I can dig through my case for a spare T-shirt or my rash guard, Jen tugs me out the door. I barely manage to grab the room key off the bedside table before we're out in the hallway. Jen leads us confidently out the front door of the hotel, past a group of wedding guests still mingling, and toward the water.

"Should we look for a pool?"

"Ocean all the way." Jen points to a pier that extends into the water, the same one we spotted from the ferry. It's far from the pier where Hannah and Eric are acting out their reunion, so it works for me. "That looks good."

"All right." We walk arm in arm, chatting easily about the island's amenities. On the way, we pass Charlie. She has her bags with her and is coming from the direction of the ferry pier, so I imagine she's only just managed to extricate herself from the bottleneck.

"Hey!" I gesture for her to come over and she does. "Want to swim with us?"

"Thanks, but I think I'll head inside and find my room. Catch you later?"

"Sure."

She pauses. "That was sweet of Eric, right?"

"Yeah." Jen nods and squeezes my arm tighter, probably trying to head off my own thoughts on that. Thoughts which I do have. That little tableau didn't seem sweet at all to me.

"Well, see you ladies later."

Charlie wends her way toward the hotel while Jen and I continue to the swimming pier.

The water is a beautiful, almost translucent, green blue. I see a few brightly colored fish below the surface. It's like a postcard of a tropical island. The air is fresh, the sun is warm on my skin, and despite the Eric-related drama, this is an almost perfect moment.

Jen doesn't take much time to enjoy the view. She leads me to the end of the pier and stops with her pink-painted toenails poking off the edge of the wood.

"There's something I haven't told you."

Her tone is casual, but my heart skips a beat. This is the tone she uses when something is terribly wrong, like in college when she overslept her calculus midterm and had to repeat the class, or a few years ago when her grandmother died.

"What's going on?" I try to match the casual tone—I should let Jen set the mood of this interaction. Jen releases my hand and turns to face me. Her dark hair is lifted slightly from her shoulders in the cool breeze and her eyes are intense.

"I hate my job." She expels a fake-sounding chuckle of laughter. "So, I'm quitting. I quit. I already gave my notice." She pauses. "And I broke up with David."

"What?" I would never have guessed this was her news. Jen smiles strangely, then turns and leaps from the pier. Her splash into the water sends spray clear up to my knees. I stand there in shock.

I believe Jen hates her job. She loves web design, but her demanding boss and the long hours have been leaving her tired and burnt out for a while. The David thing, though, is a surprise. She and David have been a version of together for years now, almost since we graduated college. They have the most casual relationship I've ever seen, often going weeks or even months without seeing each other, then spending a weekend in bed. Jen has assured me a thousand times that their dynamic is what she wants, so I'm not sure what's going on now.

"Come on!" she calls from the water.

"Come back so we can talk!" I cup my hands around my mouth to be heard over the waves.

She shakes her head, and so, with a sigh, I jump in after her. The cool water envelops me into a world without sound. I take a moment of peace underwater, watching a school of silvery fish swim by before kicking toward the surface. I'm glad I brought my goggles.

I'm worried, though. I must have missed important signals from my best friend. Since our earliest *Buddy-Up* days, we've always been there for each other. If I've missed all this just because I was distracted by my Hannah crush, I'll be really upset with myself. Thinking back on our recent conversations, she's buoyed me up whenever I've been feeling down about Hannah. I have no ground to stand on to judge Eric. Jen deserves better from her supposed best friend.

So, I swim for Jen as soon as I've emerged from the depths of my dive and grab her by her ocean-slick shoulders.

"Come on." I give her a gentle shake in the water. "Talk to me. What's happening?"

"Sorry, that was a little rude." Jen sighs. "You know I'm just not good with all this mushy stuff. I want to enjoy our time here and not get caught up on the problems in my life."

"Come on," I repeat, shaking her again. Since we're in the water, I'm moving myself as much as her. "We're best friends. Tell me what's going on."

"Okay." Jen sighs again. "Yesterday at work, I read this article about living every day the best you can. And I realized I haven't really been living. I go to work, which is okay, but it doesn't excite me anymore. And hasn't for a long time. I see David, who I like, but don't love. I know it's silly, but I realized I want the butterflies. I want to wake up excited to live my life."

"How is that silly?" I shake her once more, then pull her in for an aquatic hug. "You deserve the best. The best job, the best boyfriend, the best everything." I reflect on all she's said. "But wait, are you saying this all happened *yesterday*?"

Jen nods.

"Right before I came over to your house. And I already feel better after talking to you. I think I can steal some clients from my company and start out freelancing. And I want to be ready for love—a real, proper love, not just what David and I had. Our arrangement may have been the right thing for me for a long time, but it isn't what I want anymore."

"Wow." I smile. "I'm so proud of you, Jen. Seriously."

"Yeah." She rolls her eyes, but I can tell she's pleased. "I know you've been saying for years I needed to try something new, especially at work, and I guess I'm really going for it. We'll see if I crash and burn."

"You won't." I'm confident in Jen's abilities. "And the ten grand from this weekend will certainly help."

"Yeah, the first half is already in my account." Jen wiggles happily, then pushes away from me and dives into the water. Taking a deep breath and securing my goggles, I follow her.

The underwater world is gorgeous. Light streams in from above, illuminating a sea of dancing seaweed, colorful coral, and darting fish. One fish swims right at me, darting out of the way just in time, and I see right into his small dark eyes.

Just ahead of me, Jen swims down, her hair buoyed behind her. She gives me an underwater thumbs-up, then makes for the surface. I stay underwater for a few more seconds, hearing my heartbeat in my ears and feeling the beautiful weightlessness of being underwater. Then I follow Jen.

"There's more." Jen is still a little breathless.

"Beyond quitting your job and breaking up with your boyfriend?"

She nods while pushing a clump of wet hair out of her face.

"I'm going to need a cheaper place to live," she states matter-of-factly. "Do you still have some space in your apartment?"

"For you, definitely."

She flashes a smile, then dives back under. I'm excited to live with my best friend again, excited to work together on creating a good life for her. As I kick down after Jen, pushing the water aside with quick strokes, I confirm I have been distracted from what really matters. Yes, I like Hannah. Of course I do. But I've known Jen for years. Jen has to be—*is*—more important. So is this trip, my first real vacation in years. In a few days, Hannah will be married and that will be that. I can't let a crush on a girl who will never have me distract me from what matters. I can't.

I'm going to leave Hannah—and her wedding—alone and focus on my best friend.

"Jen!" I call before she can dive back under. "I'm really sorry. I've been a sucky friend."

Jen splashes me.

"The first step in healing is admitting you have a problem." She uses a jokingly serious tone and I know I'm already forgiven.

"I do. I've let the whole Hannah thing distract me from what really matters. Which is you."

"And our tropical vacation!"

"And our tropical vacation."

We dive back under in unison, graceful as a pair of mermaids.

CHAPTER TEN

Eric leans in, his breath warm on my ear.

"Go get changed, okay? We have a formal dinner in a few hours."

I just nod. I'm mortified. I'm not sure if I'm more upset by the fact that I wasn't dressed properly for this or by the way Eric caught me out so expertly in front of so many people. Perhaps he meant for it to be a reconciliation after us flying here separately, but it just feels like humiliation.

I look around for Meli. All I want to do is find her and ask what she meant about me deserving better, because I'm starting to believe her. Or maybe it isn't *better* that I deserve. Maybe I just deserve someone who's on the same page as me and who respects me for who I am, not for who they want me to be. Either way, I'm out of here. For the moment anyway. Bidding Eric good-bye, I hurry away.

I spot Meli quickly. I could spot her in a crowd a mile away. She's not quite that far, but she is closer to the hotel, so I guess she's already checked in. She's in a swimsuit and arm in arm with Jen as they walk briskly away from me and to the swim pier and water, heads leaned in toward each other. Neither looks back at me.

The edges of my heart curl like old paper. Meli is more or less the one person on this island I want to be with, but she has other people she cares about. I don't want to disturb them, no matter how much I'd like to talk to her right now. I try to push my desire to see Meli from my mind. They're probably just excited to get in the water, which I would be, too, if I weren't so embarrassed.

I smile and nod at the various guests and slip through the crowd as quickly as possible. I consider following Meli and Jen, but don't. I don't want to be a nuisance. Instead, I accept my room key from a bellhop near the front desk and let him lead me to my room.

I'm on the top floor in something called a bridal suite. It really is magnificent. As soon as the bellhop opens the door, I'm drawn to the window. The views over the Caribbean are spectacular. I stand there for a while watching the waves crash on the sandy beach below and the palm trees sway in a light breeze.

When I turn to thank the bellhop, he's gone, and the door is closed behind him. I forgot to tip him. *Oops.* Yet another social situation that I've mismanaged.

I'm glad to be alone, though. I take a turn around the room, running my hand over the bed with all its white fluffy pillows and examining the bathroom with the shower so big that at least six of me could fit inside. There's even an enormous bathtub, although why anyone would use it when there's an ocean outside, I'm not sure.

Oh, but this tub is lined with jets. There's a hot tub in the middle of my bathroom. *Wow.*

There's a little desk by the window, not a standard hotel desk, but an old-fashioned creation with white metal legs and a big mirror. Maybe it's a vanity. I've never used one before. I usually slap on some mascara and a bit of lip gloss in the bathroom. Now I sit on the swivel stool and gaze into the gilded mirror.

I do look like a bit of a mess. My hair is piled into a bun

with strands falling loosely around my face. My eyes look tired and extra bright with the tiredness. My Sprinkles T-shirt, although super comfy, is hardly bridal. I feel like I've been hired to play the role of a bride, just like Meli and the others were hired to be my bridesmaids. I'm not doing a great job. In books and movies, brides always seem to be blushing and full of excitement. I don't feel that way at all. Maybe it's because the proposal was so recent, or because I didn't play a big part in planning this wedding.

Or maybe it's because I'm making a mistake and rushing into this.

I startle at a knock on the door, then a smile spreads across my face. Maybe it's Meli, though how she would have found my room, I don't know. I quickly tuck some of my loose strands of hair behind my ears and throw myself an encouraging smile. I pad across the room to answer the door.

"Hey, squirt." It's Brad. My shoulders slump and he raises his eyebrows. "Were you hoping I was Eric?"

Not at all. "Sure. Want to come in?"

He takes in my room.

"Nice digs. I like the desk, just in case you want to write some emotional journal entries about the end of your girlhood."

"It's actually a vanity." I fold my arms across my chest. "Excuse you."

Brad holds up his hand. "Consider me excused."

"No offense, but what are you doing here when you could be swimming in the Caribbean?"

"What?" Brad flops onto the bed, mussing the sheets. "I can't come visit my little sis on the eve of her wedding?"

"The wedding isn't for three days." I take a seat on the vanity stool.

"Sure. Anyway, I wanted to check on you. You didn't seem all that enthused about Eric's paparazzi stunt."

I groan.

"Was I that obvious?"

"To anyone who cares about you, yes." Brad fixes me with an intense look. "Is everything okay?"

"What do you mean?" My laugh sounds fake to my ears, and I stand and cross the room to lean on the window. Hopefully, the bright sunlight streaming in will obscure my face. "Of course everything's okay."

Brad sighs. "Everyone in our family is so concerned with appearances all the time. I'd hoped that gene skipped you."

"What do you mean?"

"Mom and Dad never really cared about us." Brad shoots me an appraising look. "This *can't* be news to you. They made me play baseball so that they could talk about my games with the other military couples, because the sport I wanted, cross-country, wasn't *manly* enough. They made you do ballet so you'd grow up *feminine* and *refined*, even though you wanted to quit after about a year and started crying before practice because the bun hurt your hair and the other kids were mean to you."

I just stare at him with my mouth open.

"Really?" I had no idea he remembered all that. Brad, a few years older and so confident, always seemed so capable and independent. I didn't know he felt just as much pressure as I did.

"Hannah. Come on." He looks at me sideways, as though in disbelief. "I'm worried you're getting married because you think our parents want you to, not because you actually want to. Are you really in love with Eric? He doesn't seem like your type."

"Mom and Dad want the best for us. And you don't know Eric. He's great." The fact that I can't think of a more specific comment than *great* probably doesn't speak well for our relationship.

Brad holds up his hands in surrender.

"Okay. You know what's best for you. I just want you to know you have choices, you know?"

Half of me wants to share with Brad. I want to spill all my worries about how I might not really be in love with Eric, about how I can't stop thinking about Meli. I want to ask if he agrees my shyness isn't a fatal flaw, like Meli said. After all, he's just shown that he disagrees with other things our parents said. Then I remember.

In college, Brad and my parents visited for Friends and Family weekend. I showed them around, telling them that my friends were quite busy, but that it was nothing to worry about. The truth, of course, was that I didn't have friends.

In the afternoon of the second day, my parents went to some tea that had been arranged for parents, and Brad and I walked around campus. We passed two women who were holding hands, clearly a couple. That kind of thing was normal at my college, but not on the military bases where we'd grown up. I saw Brad's eyes following them.

"You know," Brad said once they'd disappeared down the path, "I'm glad Mom and Dad didn't see that."

"Why?" I asked, though I already knew.

"They wouldn't want you to attend this school anymore if they knew that kind of thing went on," Brad told me, waving his hand in the direction the couple went in. "And they would totally disown you if you ever did anything like that. Be careful."

Maybe Brad just meant that I should keep any parts of myself not condoned in the Bible away from my parents. But maybe he was signaling that he agreed with them in some way. If I tell Brad about my feelings for Meli and he freaks out, he could ruin everything.

I can't take that chance.

I don't even know if what I feel for Meli is real.

"Thanks, Brad." I take a deep breath and put on a pleasant

smile. "I know I do. Now, are we going to sit around in here or are we going to explore the island?"

"I was thinking of getting something to eat." Brad speaks slowly and his eyes are slightly narrowed. He must know I was brushing him off. "Apparently there's an ice cream stand with unlimited refills."

"That sounds like a recipe for disaster. I'm in. Just let me change."

I grab a sundress and sandals from my suitcase and quickly change in the bathroom. I also comb my hair and secure it with a wide headband. Then, feeling anxious about what the afternoon might hold, I add a little makeup. That should do it.

As we head into the sunshine, I instinctively look for Meli. Maybe she'll want to join us for ice cream. Sure, she walked away back at the pier, but that doesn't mean that she doesn't want to see me. Or at least, I hope it doesn't.

Brad and I follow a stone path toward the ice cream stand he mentioned. It seems like every two steps someone stops us. Most of them are friends, family, and clients of Eric's. Okay, most are clients, but there are a few of our aunts, uncles and cousins milling about. They all look a little shell-shocked. I can't blame them. I feel like I've been parachuted into a tropical paradise, too.

Despite all the people, Meli is nowhere to be found.

Then I see her. She and Jen are walking up from the beach, dripping wet and arm in arm again. It's nice that they have each other to rely on in this new place. Jen's bathing suit is beyond revealing, but Meli looks lovely in her one-piece with her curly hair loose around her shoulders.

"Hot damn," Brad says. He's checking Jen out. Again. "Let's go talk to them."

"Um, I'm not—" I want to tell him I'm not sure Meli wants to talk to me. I catch her eye and she nods a greeting but doesn't make any move to approach. This confirms my suspicions that she doesn't want to talk right now. I tug Brad's arm, but Brad misunderstands my hesitation.

"Come on, be brave." He throws an arm over my shoulder. "Be a wingman for your big bro. Let's go!"

My stomach twists into nervous knots as I let him pull us toward Meli and Jen, who have slowed to look at the offerings of a small ice cream stand. Maybe I'm overreacting. Maybe Meli really does want to talk to me.

"Hey." Brad tries to be cool, but when he goes to lean a hand on the wall next to us, he misjudges and almost topples. I giggle and Meli laughs, too. There's a surge of warmth throughout my body when our eyes meet. Jen, however, is not laughing.

"Hey," she says. She makes eyes at my brother and stands in a way that accentuates the teeny in her bikini.

"How are you enjoying the island?" Brad asks. His voice sounds totally different from the jokey tone he uses with me. It's his flirty voice. Something about that tone gives me a childish urge to laugh.

"It's not bad." Jen flips her wet hair over her shoulder and rotates a little. More of her itsy-bitsy bikini bottom comes into view. I look away, biting my lip to hide my smile. I lock eyes with Meli again.

"Hey." Meli nods to the side and we step away from Brad and Jen as they continue their courting ritual. "How are you doing?"

I am confused, tired, and worried about my wedding, but none of that seems very important with Meli standing next to me.

"Oh, you know, it's hard to not be doing well in paradise." I gesture at the cabanas and lounge chairs sprinkled across the sand. "How are you?"

"Good." She hesitates. "I'm sorry. I made things a little

weird on the boat. I figured you'd want space after I tried to meddle in your marriage, and I also realized I have been neglecting Jen. Apparently, she broke up with her boyfriend and quit her job. Yesterday." She shakes her head in wonder.

My heart melts a little. Meli wasn't really avoiding me—or she was, but for a good reason.

"How's Jen doing? Breaking up and quitting on the same day could really throw a person off."

"You know, I think she's all right." We both look back to the courting couple. Jen has one hand on Brad's arm and is bent over laughing. Her cleavage threatens to spill from her miniature bikini top.

"Maybe more than all right."

"Maybe."

"Also, not marriage."

"Huh?"

I hesitate. "I'm not married. I mean, not yet."

Something sparks in Meli's eyes. I consider running inside and breaking things off with Eric right now, just to see that expression again. But I'm still being ridiculous. Meli and I are just friends, no matter what my feelings may be toward her. I'm not married now, but I will be in a few days. It would be silly to throw away stability and my parents' lifelong dream just because Meli's beautiful brown eyes sparkle in the most intriguing way. And just because even the faintest touch from her sets every one of my nerves on end. And just because every moment I spend with her, I feel like I'm flying.

Silly.

"Right. Never having been engaged, I forget all the nomenclature. I mean, not that being engaged means you would be familiar with it. Although, I guess you would be. Right? But I just meant your future marriage." Meli is rambling again. She's adorable. I smile at her reassuringly.

"So, will you spend some more time with Jen, or do you want to do a little exploring with me?" Something about Meli's discomfort encourages me to be brave.

Meli looks to Jen and Brad, who now stand about three inches apart and are basically undressing each other with their eyes. As we watch, they turn and head toward the café. Neither spares a glance for either of us.

"It looks like Jen will be okay for an hour or two," Meli says drily. She glances down at her swimsuit and flushes. "Just let me change?"

I don't really want her to change. She is breathtaking in the swimsuit with her long, muscular legs in full view. But I nod and lean against the wall while she hurries to her room.

"*There* you are." My mother wears a very large hat and a long, modest brown dress, which looks very out of place on this beautiful tropical island. She looks at my much shorter dress, which is yellow and covered in tiny flowers, and wrinkles her nose. Perhaps she doesn't like the hem that stops above my knee. That would definitely have gotten me in trouble as a kid, and I wouldn't be surprised if the same standards apply now. "I've been looking for you everywhere."

"You have?" I'm surprised. My parents and I aren't anywhere near codependent, and I hadn't really expected to see either of them until dinner.

"Of course I have." My mom stands close beside me. "You need to be careful, sweetie."

"What do you mean?" My heart rate accelerates as ideas flash though my mind. Maybe she's worried about me standing here, by myself, when I should be with my fiancé. Maybe she thinks I'm getting too much sun before the big day. Maybe she's noticed Eric and I don't have the spark other couples do. Or she's noticed how I look at Meli. It's probably that. *Oh no.*

"That poor Eric. He's such a sweetheart, surprising you

with those flowers and the photographer, and there you were in your sweatpants looking like a fish out of water." She shakes her head and tuts. The sound recalls a flood of bad childhood memories of all the times I disappointed my parents by not being Perfect Hannah. "I hope those pictures don't get used. You can't just coast, honey. You need to make an effort with your man, or he will lose interest. Your other bridesmaid came off the ferry dressed to impress. Even Eric noticed, sweetie. How would it look to everyone if something were to happen just because you didn't put on a nicer dress and try a little harder?"

I gape at her. Apparently, the last few years of not living with my parents helped me forget how much they really do care about appearances, just like Brad said.

"Well…I'm actually…worried, maybe? I like Eric, but I don't know that I love him. Some part of me wonders if I should even go through with the wedding."

My mother raises her sculpted eyebrows. "You *must* go through with the wedding. Everyone flew all the way here to see you get married. Can you imagine the embarrassment if you didn't?"

The palm trees and cabanas close in around me. *Oh no.*

"Even if I don't love him, Mom?"

"Honey." My mother leans closer. "You might not get another chance. Eric is willing to work with all your…issues. You might not get that again. Don't throw this away."

I feel all the old pressures pushing in and I wrap my arms around my stomach.

"Honey, don't do that." My mom glances pointedly at my arms. "Take a deep breath, pull yourself together, and make this work. Okay? If you don't love Eric now, that will come later. Now, I better go find your father."

With that, she pats me on the shoulder and continues along the path. I lean against the low wall behind me, trying to steady myself. My mother had a point—I should take a deep breath. Although I doubt I should listen to any of her other advice.

I think she expected her directives would strengthen my resolve to go through with this marriage, but they had the opposite effect. Getting married because that's what my parents want no longer seems as important when it's so clear they are more interested in how things look than in how I feel.

Chapter Eleven

I hurry out of my room wearing a pair of green shorts and a tank top and scan the beach for Hannah. I don't see her anywhere, and my heart skips a beat. Maybe she changed her mind about exploring with me. Perhaps Eric pulled her away somewhere to meet business partners who will judge her if she isn't loquacious enough.

Then I see her. I almost melt with relief. She leans on the same wall as before, just a little farther down. She looks a little shocked or flustered, maybe. Behind her, Mrs. Barnes walks away with a swish in her step.

"Everything okay?" I stop beside her.

"Yeah." Hannah shoots a look at her mother's departing back, then turns to me. "My mother just had some, well, interesting thoughts. It wasn't, um, exactly what I'd hoped for. But let's not get distracted. We have exploring to do!"

I'm dying to ask what her mother said, but I hold back my questions.

"It's an adventure."

We march toward the path that leads to the beach. A few more guests try to approach Hannah, but she just smiles at them politely and keeps moving. Finally, we make it to the beach and hang a right to walk parallel to the waves. The sand is soft beneath our feet, and we walk in silence, listening to the sound of the waves and stepping around sunbathers and others splashing in the water. Despite the idyllic scenery, the mood feels heavy. Hannah is biting her lip and her arms are crossed. Maybe she isn't really in the mood for exploring, despite what she said.

"Want to follow that path?" I gesture to a narrow track that leads toward the island interior.

"Sure."

I lead the way up the second path. My thoughts race. I want to ask Hannah about her conversation with her mother, and about whether she agrees that she deserves better than Eric. I want to lighten the mood with some joke about Harry Potter or trees. I want to put my arm around her. I don't do any of that. I stay quiet, which feels like progress for me. We move into a jungly area filled with broad, lush trees. If I'd known about these towering behemoths, their leaves studded with spiky yellow orbs, I definitely would have been one in my childhood play. The shade is quite a relief.

"How's your speech coming?"

"Right! I almost forgot I'm your maid of honor."

Hannah's hand flies to her heart. "How dare you forget your fake job?"

I giggle at her exaggerated show of fake horror. "I know. I'm the worst." I grin at her, and she grins back. It's a relief she seems to have forgotten my ridiculous attempt to undermine her relationship and marriage. We can go back to our easy, normal friendship. I prefer that reality, even if it does still include me pining after her quietly in the back of my mind. I sigh internally. I'm the fake maid of honor in a real wedding where I have a huge crush on the bride.

"I was wondering, though…" I hope Hannah doesn't think I'm rude. "Who decided I'd be the maid of honor, you or Eric?"

"Good question." A mischievous smile spreads across Hannah's face, and now I can't wait to hear the answer.

"Eric really wanted Crystal to be the maid of honor. Probably because she dresses like a stripper." Hannah pauses, wrinkling her nose. "Sorry, that was mean. I should never go after another person, especially not a woman, for how she chooses to dress."

"I agree, Crystal is a little over the top, but we shouldn't make fun of how she dresses. I would more go after her strange voice and her patronizing tone."

"Oh my gosh, did you hear her ask me at the bachelorette party if I've ever seen a penis before?" Hannah clasps her hands over her eyes in horror.

"The demonstration with the cucumber that followed was much worse. I can't believe she went rummaging through your refrigerator to find that."

We burst into laughter again, scaring off a few tropical birds. I take a closer look at our surroundings. There are tall trees draped with vines, some enormous ferns, and a few little lizards and birds. I can still hear the waves crashing, but I can't see the ocean anymore. The air here smells a bit different, more alive than on the beach somehow, and maybe a bit more humid.

"Anyway," Hannah continues, once she's gotten her laughter under control, "Eric was telling me that Crystal was the *best* choice, and I was like 'Oh, definitely, you're right for sure.' And then I was like 'I'm just glad you can see past how bad it looks.' And he was like 'What do you mean?' And I was like 'That you picked the one with the biggest boobs instead of the prettiest one,' and he was like 'Wait, which one is the prettiest one?' and I was like 'Obviously Meli.'" Hannah blushes, her cheeks turning pink. "Anyway, in the end, he agreed that we should choose you."

My jaw drops at this long and eloquent story, very unlike anything I've heard from Hannah before. She must be pretty comfortable with me if she's okay with talking this much. I also like that she called me the prettiest bridesmaid, even though the context isn't exactly romantic.

"Wow, how flattering. Thank you...Did you know he still calls me Milly?"

"Yeah." Hannah wrinkles her nose. "I'm really sorry. I've been trying to correct him, but I think he thinks it's funny that I get so upset about it."

I'm annoyed all over again by Eric's behavior and about a millisecond away from asking Hannah why she stays with him. But I promised myself I wouldn't interfere with her wedding, and a question like that would be interfering, big time.

"His coworkers are just as bad. Some wedding guest grabbed me in the hallway when I was coming to meet you and asked if I could do a quick clean of his room, because he'd spilled some coffee."

"That's horrifying on so many levels." Hannah shakes her head. "I'm so sorry, Meli. Just say the word and we can escape this island."

The idea is far too tempting. "How would we even leave? The big boat is gone."

"Well." Hannah stops and leans toward me conspiratorially. "You know the giant yacht parked at the dock? The one with the blue stripe on the side? That's Eric's. He's decided we'll spend a few days on it after the wedding, a kind of mini honeymoon before we go back to work." She pauses and I watch an unhappy emotion cross her face before she shakes it off. "I bet we could steal it."

"Can you sail a yacht?"

"I mean, how hard can it be?" She holds her hands out as if grabbing an invisible wheel and turns it from side to side.

"I think that might be a race car." I reach out and wrap my hands around hers, moving them further apart and in a wider circumference. "Ship wheels are bigger, like this."

"And you know that because…"

"Because I've watched plenty of pirate movies." I smile, then realize she can't see me. I've stepped behind her and wrapped my arms around her body to demonstrate the correct hand positioning on a ship's wheel. Which I don't know either. What I do know is that she fits perfectly in my arms. Her sweet cinnamon smell washes over me again. I quickly step away and in front of her again, trying to ignore the stirring inside me. I'm definitely blushing, and my hand is halfway to my hair to pull on a strand before I realize what I'm doing and bring it back to my side. We gaze at each other in silence.

"I think that once we get on the stolen yacht, we can figure it out," Hannah says.

"Won't Eric be upset?"

"No. I think he could buy another yacht with his pocket change. He just bought a house on Martha's Vineyard to summer in. That's *summer* as a verb."

"Well, that's normal for rich people."

"No, no. This is his second house on Martha's Vineyard. The first one was *too small*. That's not to mention his house in the south of France, the condo in Manhattan, or this private island. I think there might be a few more properties."

"Is he that good a businessman?"

Hannah shrugs. "He believes he is. But he's only running the hotel chain because his parents have at least a dozen businesses around the world and decided to let him try one."

"Sure. That's how it usually goes for the privileged." I clap my hand over my mouth. I've done it again. "I'm so sorry. I don't really know that. That was prejudiced…I'll shut up."

"Well, he *is* incredibly privileged, though I also don't know how things usually go." She pauses. "You probably wonder why I'm marrying him."

"Because you love him?" I try to keep my voice neutral.

"I...well. Um. The..." She is clearly uncomfortable with the question, and I immediately lose my resolve. Maybe I don't really want to hear how she feels about Eric. Or about me.

"It's okay." I rest a hand very lightly on her forearm for a fraction of a second. "You don't have to talk about it."

"I just..." She shakes her head. "I'm sorry. I just can't..." She laughs uncertainly and waves a hand.

"We'll circle back to this if you want to." Just because I'm desperate to know what she wanted to say doesn't mean that I'm going to push her to talk when she's clearly struggling. I'm not a monster. She nods. "Okay, on to another topic, then. Cool animal facts."

Her laughter echoes in the quiet of the jungle. "Is this a topic that you know a lot about?"

"Yes." I nod decisively. "Did you know that polar bears cover their noses with their paws when they hide in the snow?"

"Oh, that's a good one." Hannah covers her nose with one hand. "Can you see me now?"

"Hannah? Where are you?" I wheel around as though she'd gone invisible.

"Wow. Very effective." She takes her hand away. "I know one. Did you know that whale blood vessels are so big that an adult could swim in them?"

"I did *not* know that. I hope no one's ever tried."

We go back and forth for a while, sharing increasingly silly facts as we stroll around the island. We make a full circuit, passing underneath the landing pad for helicopters, a smaller dock where a few modest motorboats are moored, and some smaller houses and cabins. When we reach the main beach and hotel again, Hannah sighs.

"I better go get ready for dinner. See you there?"

"See you there."

We go our separate ways. I look for Jen—I disappeared for at least an hour, and I want to make sure she's okay. When

I finally find her, she's tucked into a cabana with one leg flung over Brad's. She sees me and grins broadly. She looks as pleased as the cat who got the cream. She'd probably be happy for me to come over, but I've confirmed she's okay and I don't want to impose. Instead, I wave and continue to meander. Unlike Hannah, I don't need hours to prepare for this evening.

I think about my bridesmaid speech, a speech that's a script instead of my own words.

Eric sent me a speech that he'd had written by one of his PR people. It's all about the love he and Hannah share. According to the current version, I've known Hannah *like, totally forever* and there's one disturbing declaration of how I *like, totally want a man like Eric for myself.* When I first read it, I almost vomited from sheer revulsion.

I am not going to give that speech.

Not anymore. I was planning to. Hannah was so distant this past week, and I was convinced Eric was who she wanted. But after today, I can't bear the thought of saying those words, not even if it means losing the other half of my ten thousand dollars and my maid of honor bonus.

I walk back out onto the now-empty swimming pier and sit on the end, depositing my sandals on the wood beside me and letting my feet swing. It's beautiful here—all turquoise ocean and clear sky. There's a light breeze to cut through the heat and the sun warms my skin while little waves send sea spray toward my feet. I tilt my head up like a flower searching for the sun and plan my speech.

I will be honest. Honest enough. I want Hannah to know how special she is and that she deserves everything good in life. I want her to know that I think the world of her and that she shouldn't settle for anything. So much for not interfering in the wedding—performing a speech other than the one scripted is against my contract. After a few moments of thought, I grab my phone.

The words flow out of me onto my phone's little screen, until the low battery sign flashes. When it does, I notice the sun has started to set. Beautiful oranges and yellows and reds streak the sky. It's one of those magical moments that seems too good to be true yet somehow still lacks for being seen alone. I wish Hannah were here. I sit for a while longer. The sun drops below the horizon before I rise to go inside and change for the welcome dinner.

The welcome dinner where I'll give my speech.

When I walk into our room, Jen is already there. She's leaning over the mirror to put on lipstick. She's wearing a pair of slacks and a nice blouse, and her hair is pulled back with a thin silver band.

"Hey." Her face lights up. "Sorry for ditching you."

"Oh, please don't worry about it. For all my mooning over Hannah, I deserve a bit of ditching. Now spill! What happened with Brad?"

"Okay, okay, twist my arm." Jen tosses the lipstick onto the table and flops backward onto one of the beds, her hands behind her head. It's a position I recognize from college when she had just gotten home from a date and couldn't wait to tell me all about it. "He's so *cool*, Meli. At first, I just thought he was, you know, hot." She fans herself. "But we had a really deep conversation about our lives, what we want to be doing, family pressures. And…" She blushes. "He invited me to stay at his property in California while I figure things out. He runs a surfing school, so it's not like he's inviting me to live in his house or something, but still."

"Uh, are you going to go?" Things are changing very rapidly. Yesterday, Jen broke up with her boyfriend and quit her job. A few hours ago, she asked to move in with me. Now she's gotten an invitation to move to a surfing school. I can't help worrying about my usually levelheaded and thoughtful friend.

Jen rolls onto her stomach and looks at me intensely. "Meli, I know I asked to move in with you, and I still want to do that. I think. But when have I ever just said yes to something like this? I can freelance from anywhere if that's what I want to do. Would you be sad, though?"

"I mean, obviously I would miss you." I slowly sit next to her on the bed. "And I wouldn't want you to rush into anything just because your life is unsettled right now. But I also support you chasing what makes you happiest."

"Yeah." Jen sighs. "I guess I'm still figuring out what would make me the happiest. But living on a surfer ranch with a hot guy could certainly be a piece of it."

"It certainly could." We both giggle. "Um…" I smooth the bed with my hand.

"You want to know about the family pressure."

"Maybe. I don't know. I don't want to know anything that would be a betrayal of Hannah's privacy, but I've seen how she is with her parents. I can't imagine growing up with them was easy."

"Well, I'll tell you what Brad told me. I'd told him that I became a software designer because it was a balance of something I wanted and what my parents wanted for me. They'd always wanted me to do something technological, you know, because *technology is the future*." She uses a dramatic parent voice. I smile.

Jen flips her hair and pushes herself into a seated position. She's glossing over a lot—her story is more complicated than she wants to get into now.

"Anyway," she continues, "Brad said he was impressed I could do that. He'd basically gone as far from his parents' expectations as he could. Apparently, they don't even talk much anymore. They were really into traditional gender roles when he was a kid, and since his dad is in the military, there was a lot of pressure for him to enlist, too. And there was a lot of pressure for both him and his sister to marry and have children."

A piece of the puzzle of Hannah's marriage clicks into place. My hypothesis that she is getting married mostly because of her parents' expectations might be right. But I wonder why Brad was able to break away so completely, while Hannah still struggles with the pressures that were placed on her.

"That sounds really difficult."

"Yeah." Jen nods. "I wish that everyone could have grown up in a family like yours."

"We had our problems." I pause. "But I wish that everyone could have had a family like mine, too. I never doubted that I was loved or that my parents supported me."

We both sit in silence for a moment. Then I get to my feet.

"We only have a couple minutes before the dinner. I better get ready."

"Excited for your big speech?"

"Maybe a little nervous."

"Wow, an actor nervous about a gig in front of her smallest audience yet?"

"I don't feel like an actor right now. I'm not really playing a part anymore."

I grab a white skirt and blue top from the closet. I head to the bathroom for a quick shower, put on a little basic makeup, and get dressed. Finally, I deftly pull part of my hair back into a bun and leave the rest down. It's my signature style when I want to do something with my hair but don't have the time to do something fancy. I take a deep breath and blow it out slowly. Then I head back into the bedroom.

"Ready."

"It's incredible how quickly you get ready, but fine. Let's go."

Outside, the sun has fully set, and our path is now lit by small, glowing lanterns around knee height. The constant crashing of the ocean mixes with the hum of cicadas. Jen and I follow the winding path to a patio area filled with round tables under white tablecloths.

"This is the life," Jen says appreciatively as someone hands her a glass of champagne. "Thanks." She smiles at the waiter. "Come on, let's find our seats."

We scan the tables for our name cards and find them at a table near the front. Jen and I are sitting together, along with Charlie. There are also a few unfamiliar men's names that probably belong to groomsmen. Crystal's name isn't anywhere to be found, which strikes me as odd. Just as I'm starting to get excited at the prospect of a Crystal-free evening, though, Eric approaches.

"Chaz-alert!" I nudge Jen and she quickly swallows her crab puff and gives a fake smile.

"Milly, Jen." Eric smiles his white-teeth gleaming smile at us. "Milly, can I speak with you for a minute?"

"Sure," I say.

"Well, there's been a bit of a change of plans." Eric makes an exaggerated sad face. "See, we just thought it would be more believable for Hannah's best friend to be, well, you know." It's a good thing he isn't an actor, because he's terrible at it.

"I don't know." My voice is too high, too fake-polite. Jen's eyes widen, but Eric doesn't notice.

"More…similar to her. Anyway, Crystal was able to step up at the last minute."

"More similar to her," I repeat. "So…*white.*"

"Wow." Eric holds his hands up, laughing. "*I* never brought race into this. I—*we* just think that Crystal has more in common with Hannah. Anyway, you get paid the same, so don't worry. Just enjoy your evening! You can enjoy sitting at a chattier table, at least." He turns and strides away. Based on his light step, I bet he thinks this conversation went well.

My hands are balled into fists. I barely notice when Jen

guides me into a chair and hands me a glass of water with tiny floating slices of cucumber and lemon. I've never been more furious. *Hannah had no part in this decision.* This was all Eric. But that doesn't make it better. I can't stop fuming.

The table fills. Charlie arrives, looking refreshed and pretty in a dark pink sundress. She's followed by a group of men who I assume must be Eric's groomsmen. One of them leers at me. I roll my eyes. I can't deal with another Chaz this evening.

"You look tense." He leans toward me. "Maybe you need something stronger than water."

"Maybe." I bat my eyes at him. "I think a baseball bat could do."

He laughs uncertainly, but at least he backs off.

"Calm down," Jen hisses. "Eric is a jerk, but we knew that. If you don't take a deep breath or two, things are really going to go downhill."

"Fine." I take a deep breath and exhale. I can't let my temper get the best of me, despite ample provocation. "You're right. I'm just going to sit here. Calmly."

Jen looks at me warily but doesn't say anything. I do what I said I would, though. I sit quietly, hands balled into fists, furious. I don't get to give my speech. I probably won't get to speak with Hannah at all tonight. And Eric has continued to play the role of the villain pitch-perfectly.

Without the chance to give my speech, I'm not sure what to do. I could try to pull Hannah to the side to say what I want, but I'm guessing she'll be at Eric's side most of the night. I might have to wait until tomorrow to get another moment with her—and tomorrow might be too late. The wedding is fast approaching, and Hannah still seems to think that Eric is her only future. She needs to know that isn't true.

Chapter Twelve

Oh my God, Eric, that's so funny!" Crystal is in full form today, dressed in a skintight leotard and miniskirt. She sits to my left, while Eric is on my right, but she keeps leaning across me to talk to him. I'm invisible. I'm the bride, but if I vanished right now, I doubt Eric would even notice. Not that I really mind—I don't think I could have brought myself to talk to Crystal anyway, even if she'd wanted me to.

On Eric's other side is his best man, Hunter. Hunter is on his third glass of a bright red liquid that has him extremely tipsy. I glance over at Meli's table. I wish she were here beside me. She could transform this whole situation from humiliating nightmare to funny incident in a heartbeat. But she *isn't* here. Eric said she changed her mind about being my maid of honor at the last minute, which I know is a lie. Meli wouldn't do that.

I glance at the dessert. It's a bowl full of meringue dyed blue, perhaps to look like the ocean—if you had no concept of what the ocean looks like. I have no interest in eating it. The only good thing about dessert is that it signals the end of the meal. I just need to get through the speeches, and I'll have survived.

As if reading my mind, Eric taps his fork against his glass, drawing everyone's attention.

"Okay, I think we have a few speeches prepared. Who wants to go first?"

"Me!" Crystal shoots to her feet, raising her hand. Eric waves to her to continue, and she beams. "Well, you guys, I have known Hannah, like, totally forever and I can promise I've never seen her as happy as she is now. I mean, who wouldn't be with a guy like Eric? I could like totally use a real man like him myself." She winks and I wonder if it's part of the script or something she threw in for fun. Either way, I want to either roll my eyes until they fall out of my head, or just leave. Preferably the latter. This is so embarrassing, and I'm upset with Eric for putting me through this—and at Crystal for agreeing to it. Surely, if Meli were my bridesmaid, she wouldn't be giving this speech.

"Hannah is totally shy and quiet, but she's a real sweetie." *And you're a real fake.* "She's the kind of person who, like, gives someone else the last cookie and would never say something mean."

I almost laugh because this isn't true. I'm not exactly a sweetie in my own head. And I only willingly give away the last cookie when it's not a good kind of cookie.

Crystal's speech wends its way past a few manipulated childhood stories I passed to Eric's PR person for this occasion and ends with another hint Crystal could use a guy like Eric. I wonder if he inserted that into the speech. I wouldn't put it past him.

I think so little of Eric. I wouldn't be surprised if he put little notes in the speeches to make himself look good. He's never been anything but horrible to Meli. Lately, I can't be around him without feeling a seething rage in some deep, buried part of me where I feel that kind of emotion.

Oh no. I've made a huge mistake.

I thought I could live with Eric and all his problematic qualities because I didn't feel like I had any other options. I was supposed to get married. I was supposed to be a wife. But now I realize that I do have a choice—*right now*. I can choose myself and my own happiness over what other people want for me. It feels almost impossible to extricate myself from the mess I've gotten myself into, but I still have a chance to change everything.

I sit through the rest of the speeches, clapping politely at Hunter's revelation on how much of a player Eric used to be and how Hunter never thought he'd settle down. Then my dad speaks to what a great wife and mother I'll be. The whole time, this indescribable feeling keeps building inside me. I've never embraced it before.

I think it could be bravery.

After the speeches, people get out on the dance floor and wiggle around and jump like they're sugar-high toddlers up after bedtime. Meli and Jen dance together. Their laughter descends into hilarity as their moves get sillier and sillier. Charlie shimmies with a group of my young cousins, all the while turning down advances from several of the groomsmen. She's very good at redirecting them.

"Let's dance." Eric's voice is soft in my ear. I let him pull me to my feet and onto the dance floor, where he grabs me by the waist and starts thrusting his hips around. I've never been big on dancing at all, at least not like this. There are strobe lights flashing, the music is too loud, and Eric's dance moves are too aggressive for me. Maybe him being around his old friends and drinking has made him too bold. I grab his hands for the fourth or fifth time to stop them from wandering toward my butt. I could use a lesson from Charlie on avoiding this kind of dancing.

"Hey, come on! It's only two days until the wedding anyway!"

"Can we talk?" My heart is in my throat, but there's no way I can back down now. I look over at Meli, still laughing and dancing, and for a moment, our eyes meet. Maybe I'll have a chance with her. Maybe I won't. But that doesn't matter, either.

What matters is that I finally do the right thing, for myself and for a person I think I could love.

Okay, it matters if I get a chance with Mel. It matters a lot. But that's not why I'm doing this.

"I like the sound of that!" Eric pulls me away from the dance floor and onto the path to the hotel. I redirect us toward the pier. Of course he grumbles a little, but he follows me.

"Why are we leaving the party if not to…spend a little time in private?" He's more drunk than I've ever seen him.

"We're leaving the party because we need to talk, Eric."

"Hannah, come on! We've talked about this. You can't leave social situations just because you feel a little uncomfortable."

"Right. Here is fine." I can't wait any longer. I pull him down next to me on a bench overlooking the ocean. As I turn to him, I try to school my features into a sympathetic expression. "Eric, I, um, I've made a mistake. This is all a mistake. I c-can't marry you. I'm sorry."

He seems unfazed. "Cold feet?"

I shake my head. "It's more than that…I think that I'm interested in, um, girls." It's the first time I've said it aloud, and I still couldn't get the word *lesbian* over my lips, but it's progress. It seems kinder, anyway, than to say that even if I did like guys, there's no way I would like him, knowing what I know now. I've just seen too much of Bad Eric over the last month to let this continue another minute.

There's a long pause.

"Are you sure?"

"I mean, pretty sure."

"But we haven't even slept together." His hand now roams toward my thigh, and I scoot away. "You might like it. You can't just dismiss what we have without trying it." He pauses. "I think I get it, though. This is part of your social anxiety, right? Come on, Hannah, just relax for two seconds and let me help you."

"No." I keep my voice as firm as I can, and I push his

broad, too-warm hand off my leg. I wanted to be nice about this, but maybe nice isn't the way to go. "This is about me being interested in women, not in you."

"Okay." Eric sighs. "It isn't what I wanted, but we can still make this work."

"What?"

"Yeah." He shrugs. "You need someone who can provide a cover of respectability in front of your family. I need a pretty, quiet, wholesome girl to stand next to me at social functions. And we get along fine. We can be married in name but see other people." His eyes brighten a little. "You can bring women to the house. And I still think that one night with me would change your mind."

If the days haven't worked, one night will not make a difference.

"No. That's not what I want, all right? I want love and trust and partnership. Even if that means going against what my parents want or what you want." I can't believe I'm saying this out loud, and with such confidence, but I also know it's true. And I know it's time to stand up for myself. It's past time, really.

Then I realize something else. "You were planning to sleep around even if we got married, weren't you?"

Eric has the grace to look a little sheepish.

"I like you, Hannah, but you're a little vanilla for me. And very submissive. Which can be fun, but you know..." It all makes sense. The glances, the obvious flirting, the way she was promoted to maid of honor at the last minute.

"Crystal." The sheepishness grows in Eric, along with what I detect as pride in his expression. My resolve to end this relationship, this charade, right now, intensifies. I should have known that something was going on with Crystal. Even my mother noticed something between them. I was just too caught up in my own head to recognize it.

"She is hot. If you think you're a lesbian, you must recognize that."

"Wow." I shake my head. I can't stand to be around this man for even one more second. "You insulted me, you were already cheating on me before we were even married, and you don't seem apologetic at all. All of which is on top of the fact that I'm not attracted to you. I'm leaving."

"Hannah!" Eric seems mildly alarmed for the first time in our conversation. "You can't do that. I love you and stuff. What are people going to think?"

I wave my hand in dismissal.

My family may be disappointed, but ultimately, they'll be fine.

Or they won't.

It's my life.

"You can tell them whatever you want. I really don't care, because I doubt I'll see these people again. Plus, the people I really care about see through you already."

I pause to look at Eric. He's the same man who seemed sweet and accommodating when we first started dating, but I know that was just a veneer. If Eric actually loved me, breaking up with him would be very difficult. But now it's the easiest thing I've ever done.

"Bye, Eric."

I get up, smooth my skirt, and leave without a glance back. Eric shouts after me, something about enjoying my life as a hermit and not seeing a good thing when it was staring me in the face. I want to shout back that I will enjoy my life, and that I'm plenty good at recognizing good things, but it isn't worth the breath. I just speed up until I'm almost jogging, then running. I'm worried about Eric following me, but that isn't why. Instead of running away from Eric, I'm running toward something.

Maybe even someone.

My parents are never going to talk to me after this. I can

be almost sure of that. And I hardly care. I love them, but trying to live up to their expectations brought me to the very brink of being trapped in a loveless marriage with a total jerk for the rest of my life.

I'm done with that.

I'm inside the hotel. I run to my room first, knowing that's where people will look for me, and shove my passport, toiletries, and clothes into my carry-on. I strip off my evening gown with relish and replace it with a pair of sweats and my Sprinkles top. I dare anyone to say that it's inappropriate for the situation now.

Then I'm running again, passing a few bewildered-looking guests. I wave to them politely, ignore their questions, and keep going. I have places to be.

It's time to tell Meli how I feel. As much as that scares me. As much as I can't imagine how I'm going to put my feelings into words when she's looking at me with those beautiful brown eyes. It's time to be brave.

CHAPTER THIRTEEN

I'm dancing with Jen, both of us flailing around like chickens with our heads cut off, when I see Eric lead Hannah by the hand into the darkness. My stomach clenches and, just like that, I've lost all my interest in dancing. It isn't my place to interfere, but I can't stand the thought of them together. It's not even jealousy—well, mostly not. I am truly worried for Hannah.

"What's going on?" Jen follows my gaze as Hannah's skirt disappears around a palm tree, then turns back to me and makes a sad face. "I'm sorry."

I shrug. "Whatever. But I think I'm going to head back to the room."

"What?" Jen shakes her head. "You can't go mope in our room, okay? I forbid it."

"I'm not going to mope. I'm just going to read a little and relax. Even I have my limit of how much I want to be around people. Plus, I think there's someone else who wants to dance with you." I nod to Brad, who stands with a blue drink in each hand, trying to catch Jen's eye. When she sees him, she blushes crimson and does a little bobble head maneuver.

"Is it really…"

"Yes, it's fine." I give her a little shove toward Brad. "Go."

"You are literally the best." Jen gives me a very uncharacteristic hug and bounces toward Brad.

I shake my head, smiling, then trudge toward my room. I told Jen I wasn't going to mope, but I am. That's the struggle of having the world's biggest crush on the world's straightest girl. It's only seven in the evening, but I'm going to watch old *Firefly* episodes on my phone and eat my secret stash of chocolate that I hid in the mini fridge—not that it was a particularly clever hiding spot. I deserve an evening of chocolate and comfort TV.

Back in my room, I change into my polka dot pajama pants and an overlarge Guns N' Roses T-shirt with the band's name in giant letters across my chest. It belonged to my dad before me, and it always makes me feel better. I climb into my bed, pull the covers up, and reach for my phone. Fictional world with a cute mechanic and plenty of adventures, here I come.

About a half an hour later, I'm watching Kaylee bounce down a flight of metal stairs. *Wow, I definitely have a type. I should probably watch something else*. My mental comparison of the similarities between Kaylee and Hannah is cut off by a knock on the door. It's probably Jen without her key. *Great*. I shove the covers off to answer the door.

It's Hannah, with a bag over her shoulder.

She's back in her Sprinkles top, her hair tied back in a messy bun. She still wears her nice makeup from the evening, but she looks much more comfortable. She looks much more like herself. She's beautiful. She beams and shifts from foot to foot with either excitement or nerves, I'm not sure. Her fingers interlace and slide apart a couple of times before she speaks.

"Hi." She waves with both hands, then peers into the room behind me. "I hope I'm not interrupting anything."

"No, no, you're good. Um, what's up? I thought you were somewhere with Eric."

"Can I come in?"

I gesture for her to enter. Immediately, I regret my welcome. I'm fairly neat, but my bed is strewn with chocolate and Jen's is covered in every single bathing suit she owns, which is about twenty, plus a few pairs of lingerie.

"Um, which bed is..."

"You have to ask?" My laugh is a little forced. "The chocolate bed. Sorry for the mess."

"It's okay." She kicks off her sandals and sits on the edge of my bed. The sight gives me palpitations—yes, I say *palpitations* like a grandmother. I carefully perch on the far side of the bed. "I...Eric, he..."

"You don't have to tell me."

Hannah holds up her slender hand. "I want to. I just need a minute." She takes some deep breaths. "I, well...I broke up with Eric."

"What?" I'm certain I've misheard her. Or that I fell asleep mid-episode and am now dreaming. Even though this is what I wanted, as much as I tried not to, I never really believed she would break up with Eric.

She nods, hands back to clasping and unclasping. She seems very anxious, and I wonder why. Maybe she's upset about her breakup with Eric. Or maybe she wants to be with me and is nervous to say so.

Don't be an idiot, Meli. Just because she doesn't love that jerk doesn't mean she's into you.

"Yeah."

"May I ask why?"

"Yeah...Well, it didn't help that he was cheating on me... With Crystal."

I should just let her talk, but—

"I'm so sorry. That's messed up. And Crystal? Not the choice I would have made."

"Yeah." She chuckles, her hands still kneading, her gaze fixed on the air conditioner remote on my bedside table. "It made things easier, actually. I realized I *do* deserve better. And so does Eric." She pauses. "He should have someone who can love him."

Now I'm the one who's speechless. I've forgotten all my lines. I want to ask why she can't love him, but she moves on before I can decide if that's a great or a terrible idea.

"I'm actually here to ask you something. It's…Well, you can…" She waves a hand and I wait patiently for her to put the words together. "You can say no. I…"

"Okay." Anticipation blooms in my chest. For a minute, I hope she's going to revisit the kiss conversation, although I don't know why she would.

"It's weird. Yeah, so…"

She's struggling in a way she really hasn't before with me. My first instinct is to jump in and say that she doesn't have to tell me anything, but I hope we're past that by now. I stay quiet. Maybe if I give her space and time without pushing, she'll be able to say what she wants.

Hannah bites her lip. "Maybe I can…write it?"

I grab the hotel stationery and pen from the bedside table and hold it out to her. I'm impressed by the idea. It makes sense. She is a copywriter—writing may be easier for her.

Hannah scribbles for almost a full minute before returning the notepad. I get jumpy with impatience while waiting, but I take deep stage breaths and try to remain calm. Once she finally hands the pad over, I can see that she's revised her words, erasing some parts and trying again. The letters are tiny to fit on the small pad. The message almost doesn't sound like her.

Meli, I asked around about ways to leave the island. Apparently, there's a small ferry to Saint Mary for staff leaving at 8. I'm going to go—I can't stay here. It's weird to ask, and you can say no, but do you want to come with me?

I've barely finished reading before I'm nodding.

"Yes. Give me five minutes to pack."

"Really?" Hannah looks so incredulous I want to give her a hug and shout that *of course* I'll go with her. I'd follow her to the ends of the earth. I don't, though. Just asking must have been very stressful and she seems flustered, so I'm not sure a hug would be welcome. "What about your bridesmaid pay?"

"This is more important." I'm already shoving my phone, charger, passport, and chocolate into my suitcase.

"Okay." She blushes pink. Her hands have stopped their maneuvers.

Minutes later, we walk the beach road to the small dock we spotted earlier, which we now know is for the staff transports. The flashing lights from the party behind us illuminate the sky ahead, and the loud music almost shakes the trees around us.

"I guess Eric's keeping the party going." Hannah glances back.

"Second thoughts?"

"Gosh, no." Hannah shakes her head vehemently. "I'm worried about where we're going to sleep. I'm worried about what my brother will say. But I'm *not* sad that I'm leaving. I just wish I'd broken up with Eric the moment I realized he's a jerk."

"I'm glad." Then I realize I've forgotten something—someone—very important. "Shit! Jen." And after my big words about being more present for her, too. I'm a terrible friend.

"Oh!" Hannah stops in her tracks. "Do you need to go back?"

"No, but maybe she wants to come. Let me call her." I dial Jen's number.

"What heartbreaking thing has your straight crush done now?"

I thank my lucky stars she isn't on speakerphone.

"Hannah broke up with Eric." I can now see the dock ahead.

My instinct is to hurry, but Hannah is beside me, and there's a chance we'll have to go back for Jen. "We're leaving the island. Do you want to come?"

"Well, the drama here might be entertaining," Jen says lightly. She lowers her voice, and I can hear the feeling behind her next sentence. "And, you know, maybe I can see where things go with Brad. Do you need me?"

I think she really likes Brad from the way she said that, and my heart swells with happiness for her.

"Nope. Love ya!" I disconnect and grab Hannah's hand.

"Let's go!" Ten steps into our rush to the dock, I realize I probably shouldn't be holding Hannah's hand. But she doesn't let go, so neither do I.

An elderly man is just untying the rope that anchors a small motorboat to a large metal hook. There are several staff members on board looking tired and ready to be home.

"Please wait!" I wave. He looks surprised, but he stops and lets us approach him. "Can we have a ride to Saint Mary?"

He shrugs and names a price. Thankfully I brought cash, I hand over the amount he requests. He gestures for us to climb aboard. I help Hannah into the boat, then she helps me, and we take a seat on the floor of the boat near the bow. I'm pressed against her side from knee to shoulder, and my body soaks in the contact like a desert in the rain.

The man leaps nimbly on board and takes a seat in the stern, where he starts the engine and steers away from the island. As we travel beyond the harbor, the motor's growling *put-put* washes over me. It's reassurance that we're really leaving together and sounds like the most beautiful noise in the world just now.

"Meli." Hannah's voice is soft in my ear. "Do you think this is safe?"

"A rickety motorboat making a two-hour crossing in the dark? Sounds safe to me." Then I sense she truly is nervous, and I bump my shoulder lightly against hers. "I'm sure it's fine. If it's good enough for these folks to do every day, it's good enough for us."

When she doesn't respond, I glance over and see that she's smiling ever so slightly, her gaze directed up. There's a beautiful array of stars spread across the sky. The slivered moon is not bright, but as we get farther away from the flashing lights of Saint Sofia, the stars seem to glow.

"Everything *is* going to be okay if we have a view like this," Hannah says.

I take a deep breath of the fresh sea air. I have to agree. It's a little chilly here on the water, but with Hannah's arm against mine, the stars above, and splashes of the waves on the sides of the boat, it's almost perfect.

I can't believe that we actually made it off the island. Even more unbelievably, Hannah broke up with Eric. Pride warms my heart. Breaking up an engagement would be hard for anyone, but even harder for a woman who struggles to order a drink in a restaurant or speak her mind in front of her own family.

I tilt my head back, looking at the sky. "Do you know any constellations?"

"Of course. Those, right there"—she points to a cluster of bright stars almost directly overhead—"are the three rabbits. The rabbits were adventurers and one day, they ventured out of their burrow in a big meadow to go exploring. On their journey, they came to the beach and befriended a group of passing sea turtles."

"Really?" I blink at the stars. I thought I knew a couple of constellations, but I never heard this one. Then I hear Hannah giggling. She's a good storyteller.

"Of course not, I just made that up. I can't believe you bought it."

I put my face in my hands and shake my head in an

exaggerated gesture of defeat. I am the opposite of defeated, though. Hannah's quiet laugh sends a wave of happiness and hope through me.

"You got me. Okay, but I actually know some constellations. Over there"—my shoulder brushes hers as I point—"is the ancient vase. It's named after a special vase the Greeks used to store rice and other grains." Hannah looks at me, her blue eyes glinting with suspicion.

"That's boring enough to be true, but I feel like you're making it up."

"I am."

Almost an hour flies by as we quietly exchange the names of increasingly outrageous constellations with ever more unbelievable backstories. I'm just wrapping up a tale about a one-legged snake and a mole princess that has Hannah in silent stitches when I see the lights of Saint Mary rising from the darkness.

"I think we're almost there."

"I'm getting worried again." Her smile seems a bit strained. "What are we going to do when we get there?"

"Easy. We'll ask around for a vacant room and spend the night. In the morning, we'll decide what to do next."

"You make it sound easy."

It's anything but. Finding a hotel in the late evening on an island we've never been to may not be the easiest task in the world, but if simplifying the hotel-finding process is helpful right now, then that's what I'll do. All I want to do is protect Hannah and make sure she knows she made the right decision by leaving her wedding.

When the boat docks, the rest of the passengers disembark quickly. I can't blame them. It's just after ten at night, and if I had a place to go, I'd be hurrying off, too. Instead, Hannah and I walk toward town. We pop into each hotel to ask about available rooms, but they are all booked. Apparently, we've come to Saint Mary at a very busy time of the year. There are a lot of spring breakers out and about. A group of them pass us, slurring and tripping over each other and making catcalls to lampposts.

"Well," Hannah's voice is half glum and half joking, "I guess we'll be sleeping here." She gestures to a pair of benches overlooking the ocean.

"Oh, man. I was hoping for a nice cardboard box."

Hannah shrugs. "You win some, you lose some. Let's try one more. That one looks nice. The one up those steps with the blue door."

We climb a long set of winding stone steps to the Blue Door Bed and Breakfast. Inside, a young man is just closing reception. His nametag reads *Laurence*.

"Sorry to bother you!" I hurry over. "I know you're about to close, but do you happen to have any room?"

"Actually, we had a last-minute cancelation." I barely notice Laurence's lovely lilting accent with my excitement at the news. "It's better for one person, though."

"Why?"

"It's an attic room with only one small bed." I glance at Hannah. Sharing a bed with her, if that was something she wanted, would be wonderful. But she's already been through a lot today and I would never want to put her in an uncomfortable position by suggesting that we just share it. She nods without hesitation, though.

"Okay, we'll take it."

"Perfect." Laurence is surprisingly kind given it's past the time his shift was supposed to end. I feel bad for inconveniencing him.

"The first night will be…" He checks a list, then names a very reasonable price. "I'll collect your paperwork and be right back." He disappears into a side room.

"I'll get the first night, at least." Hannah pulls out a credit card. "And let's leave an extra tip since he was closing up when we got here."

"Agreed, I was thinking the same thing. I have a bit of cash to cover the tip."

Hannah nods. Laurence reenters with a clipboard.

"Sorry for arriving just as you were leaving." Beside me, Hannah nods.

"No worries." He smiles at us. We complete the payment process, along with the tip.

Next, Laurence slides over the clipboard, which has a small form attached. When I've completed it, he hands over a key. Remarkably, it's a real key attached to a small pink shell.

"Breakfast is included and it's from seven to ten. Your room is upstairs on the third floor."

I thank him and Hannah gives him a small smile and a wave. We climb the wooden stairs, which are so narrow that there are only a few inches of space on either side of my shoulders. It's not like any hotel I've seen before.

"If it wasn't so charming, this would be very strange," Hannah mutters. She lifts her hands slightly to brush the walls on either side, emphasizing the close quarters.

"Definitely." We reach the top floor, which has just one door. I'm a little worried about the room. This could be even worse than the little cave Jen and I shared at Eric's hotel. But the door swings open to reveal an absolutely adorable little space. There are no windows on the walls, but two enormous skylights give us a spectacular view of the night sky. The walls are painted a cheerful yellow. The bathroom, just visible through an open door, looks spacious enough. And there are chocolates on the pillows of the single bed.

Here we go.

Hannah drops her bag on the floor and does a little happy dance, looking like she just won a grand lottery sweepstakes.

"We made it!"

"We made it." I hold out my hand and she returns my fist bump with enthusiasm. Then she turns to explore the room. I see her eyes land on the single bed, with its colorful bedspread and chocolate-adorned pillows.

"I can sleep on the floor, Hannah."

Hannah looks at me like I've grown a second head. "The floor is wood, there's no way it would be comfortable. This will be fine. Unless…if you'd be uncomfortable…"

"No, no." I square my shoulders. "It won't be uncomfortable for me. I was just worried about you."

"Why?" The question is completely guileless. It's hard to believe she hasn't figured out how I feel about her by now. It's not like I've been subtle.

"Well, I wouldn't want you to think I was making the moves on you." I wave my arms from side to side to represent *the moves*, although I'm pretty sure I look more like a drunken octopus.

"You wouldn't want me to think that you're making the moves on me." Hannah stands in the middle of the room, with her arms now crossed over her stomach. She looks deeply uncomfortable, and I know why. When she agreed to share the bed, she didn't properly consider that she'd be sharing it with *me*. Now she wants a way out.

"That's right. And if it would help, I really am happy to sleep on the floor."

"I…Meli…it's just…"

"It's fine." I give her a big smile and grab one of the pillows and the extra blanket off the bed, sending the pillow chocolate flying in my haste. I drop the pillow on the floor and plop down on it a little too hard. "See? Comfy."

"Okay." Hannah's shoulders slump. "If that's what you want. I'm going to take a quick shower."

She grabs her bag and disappears into the bathroom. A

moment later, the water is running and I drop my head into my hands. That couldn't have gone any worse. Hannah is so uncomfortable she can't seem to get words out, and now I get to sleep on the floor, which is hard and cold. I sigh. I rub my eyes, then reach for my bag and phone. I have several texts from Jen asking how things are going and telling me that Eric still hasn't made any announcements about Hannah's absence. Ryan sent a message telling me that they miss me at rehearsals and that he wants pictures from paradise. My dad sent a meme about dogs—he just discovered Instagram—and my mom forwarded the title of a book she thinks I should read. I spend a few minutes replying to messages, but I'm so distracted by thoughts of Hannah in the shower that I keep sending autocorrect typos. After telling Ryan that I have left the *welding* but that I'm doing *gold,* I give up.

We're in this tiny room together. I wonder what will happen when she comes out of the shower. It might just be pure awkwardness, but I hope it isn't. I hope that the moment of real connection we shared when she asked me to come with her will continue.

When the water shuts off and the door of the bathroom opens, I don't look up until Hannah pokes me lightly on the shoulder. Then I raise my head to the vision of her in a pair of pajama shorts and a top, with her hair wet around her shoulders. Her usual cinnamon scent is there, complimented by a fresh soapy smell.

"How was your shower?"

"Okay. Come here, please." She pulls me to my feet. With a hand on my back, she propels me into the bathroom. I try not to think about how she's half-naked and *so close.*

"Is this your subtle way of telling me I smell?"

She shakes her head and points to the mirror. In the condensation, she's traced a message.

Please sleep on the bed.

"I don't want you to sleep on the floor, though."

"That's not—" Hannah shakes her head and adds two more words in small letters.

With me.

"Oh." Warmth rushes through me. My knees are suddenly weak. I prop one hand on the bathroom counter for strength.

"Sorry." Hannah's voice is quiet and sounds unsure. "If you don't want to, you don't have to. But I would like…I…" She gestures to the mirror again.

"Hannah, of course I'll sleep on the bed. With you. That sounds good. I mean, I'll never turn down a chance to have a better night's rest. I'm not some sleep-hating weirdo!" *What a lovely save, Meli.* I cap off the whole discursive disaster with a double thumbs-up. Not my best performance.

Perfect. I'm still blowing this. I want Hannah to feel comfortable with me, but instead I'm probably pushing her away.

Still, Hannah wants me to share a bed with her.

"Great." Hannah looks relieved. "Well, I'm going to lie down." She leaves the bathroom.

I stand there for a few more minutes. As I stare at Hannah's message in the steam, I will my heartbeat to slow. Usually, when the adrenaline rushes through me, I am onstage with rehearsed lines in which to pour all that energy. My unscripted game will never win me a Tony.

Well, at least my heart rate is back to normal.

I venture into the bedroom to grab the bag with my toothbrush and pajamas.

Hannah's already in bed with the blankets pulled up to her waist, reading on a Kindle. Waiting for me.

I brush my teeth, take a quick shower, and change into my pajamas. Then I give myself a little silent pep talk in the still slightly steamy mirror. I can do this. I just have to be chill and casual, like anyone sharing a bed with a friend.

Back in the room, I put my phone to charge, then very slowly slide under the covers. Once there, I lie stiffly on my back, arms crossed over my stomach. Beside me, Hannah is in a similar position. *Great.* This is very conducive to a peaceful night's rest for both of us.

I reconsider the floor, but Hannah wants me to be here. For some reason.

So, here I'll be.

"Good night," Hannah says.

"Good night."

We lie there for what feels like hours, both looking at the ceiling, neither of us speaking. Finally, Hannah's breath evens out into the steady rhythm of sleep. A few minutes later, I close my eyes to listen.

Chapter Fourteen

I wake up in Meli's arms.

I'm not sure how it happened. When we went to sleep, we were both on our backs, stiff as boards. Now we face each other, one of my legs between hers, my head on her shoulder, her arm slung over my hip.

I am curled far closer to Meli than I ever was to Eric, and I don't want to move. Ever. She smells sweet, like hotel shampoo and something essentially *Meli.* Her skin is so soft and warm against mine, and my lips are just inches from her neck. I don't ever want to move. Being here with her, in her arms, feels so incredibly *right.*

Pull it together. Meli seemed hesitant to share a bed with me. It doesn't matter how good she smells or how soft her skin is. It's creepy that I'm watching her sleep.

"Meli?" I very gently shake her shoulder, and her eyes flutter open. Her hair, usually curly, is an amazing mass of ocean waves. There's a pillow crease on her cheek, but she looks more beautiful than ever.

"Hannah?" She reaches for me and pulls me closer. "This is a nice dream." Then her eyes flutter the rest of the way open, and a look of panic crosses her lovely features. "I'm really sorry!"

"It's okay." I want to say that it was more than okay, but I don't. I'm starting to worry. Maybe I was inappropriately pushy when I suggested that Meli share the bed with me. Yet another example of my prowess in social situations. We simultaneously roll out of bed and then share an awkward laugh.

"I'll just shower really quick." Meli grabs her bag and heads to the bathroom; her bare feet are loud on the wooden floor. I sink back onto the bed and run a hand through my hair. Since she just showered last night, this could be more about getting space from me than actual hygiene.

This uncertainty has to stop. No matter how Meli feels, she isn't going to say anything. She's too worried about me. Or she doesn't like me. There's no way to know either way unless I talk to her.

It has to be me who initiates the conversation.

But when Meli comes out of the bathroom, her hair in wet curls around her shoulders, I can't. Not yet. This feels like such a perfect moment, and I don't want to ruin the ease we've built. So instead of admitting my feelings or just pulling her into my arms, I say the first thing that pops into my head.

"Breakfast?"

"Yes, please!" Meli rubs her stomach dramatically. "I'm starving."

Moments later, we squeeze down the narrow staircase to the hotel's small dining room. A few other guests already sit at small round tables and sip from colorful mugs. Most of them wear the sunglasses and camera straps that identify them as tourists, but a few are dressed more casually and could be locals.

Meli and I slide into seats across from each other at one of the open tables. As if we've summoned him, Laurence appears, sliding us two mugs.

"This is traditional Saint Marian cocoa tea," he states proudly.

"Thank you." Meli smiles at him, and we both wait for him to leave, but he just stands there. His hands are clasped behind his back, and he looks at us with an expectant expression. After a beat, I realize he's waiting for us to try the cocoa tea. I look at Meli and pick up my cup. She catches on and we both quickly take sips. It's delicious—not sweet, but gently chocolatey.

"Wow, that's great." Meli nods approvingly at the mug and Laurence turns his attention to me. Oh no. He expects my feedback, too.

"Delicious." I present a slightly awkward thumbs-up. He smiles and disappears into another room.

"So." Meli curls her hands around the mug and breathes in the steam as she fixes me with an intense expression. "What would you like to do today?"

"I was thinking we could stay on Saint Mary." I hear the nervousness in my voice. "Our flights back aren't for another five days, and when we do leave, we'll leave from here. I…you can obviously go back if you want."

"Why would I do that?" Meli gestures at the quaint little breakfast room and the view of a jungle-covered hillside and crashing waves out the window. "If I can have a week in paradise, I'm not going to give that up. Do you want to find another hotel, though?"

I shake my head and take a long drink of cocoa tea. I like this hotel. I like the small bed we share.

"So, do you want to go exploring today?" Her eyes have taken on an excited gleam. "I know nothing about Saint Mary, but it may well be time to find out."

"Yes, please." I nod enthusiastically. "I'm sorry you're going to miss out on swimming with the dolphins today."

"Please." Meli rolls her eyes. "I would take hanging out with you on a cool island over swimming with dolphins on that island full of rude people. And a few good people, of course."

"Eric is more than rude, isn't he?" I shake my head. "He is racist, sexist, a cheater, and generally unaccommodating. I'm sorry, Meli. I know all of this never should have gone so far, but

I just...I just got caught up trying to be the person my parents want me to be. I thought I had only one path and that I'd better make the best of it."

Meli is quiet for a long moment. "Well, yeah. The things Eric says and does are extremely offensive."

"I know." My stomach twists. "The thought that I stood by and let him say the kinds of things that he did, especially about you..."

Meli reaches for my hand across the table. "Eric probably chose you because he knows that you struggle socially and would find it nearly impossible to stand up to him. He was manipulative. And you loved him, which made things complicated, I'm sure." Meli meets my eyes, her fingers intertwined with mine. "If you want to talk more about this, I'm here."

"I didn't love him." I tried to tell her before, but I got too nervous. "I—"

"Here are some local Saint Marian fruits!" Laurence is back. He bears a plate filled with sliced mangos, long curls of fresh coconut, whole tiny bananas, triangles of pineapple, and a few fruits I've never seen before. He sets the plate down with care, then adds a plate of pastries next to it. "Please enjoy and let me know if you need anything."

We do enjoy. The fruits are delicious—sweet, juicy, and flavorful. I eat two or three mangos on my own, slice after slice, as the juice drips down my wrist. As we eat, we're caught up in conversation about our food.

"What is this white stuff?" Meli holds a brown seed surrounded by a soft white outer layer.

"No idea. Try it."

She does. "It's very sweet."

"Hey, did you try the papaya?"

"Never. I don't like them."

"I don't know if we can hang out anymore..."

We don't even touch the pastries. Half an hour later, filled to bursting with fresh fruit and cocoa tea, we spill onto the street. It's warm outside, but not terribly hot. There's a salty breeze up from the ocean that makes the palm trees sway and rustle above our heads.

"Down to the beach or up to the jungle?" I look up and down the street.

"Let's start with the beach."

So, off we go, descending the long flight of stairs we climbed yesterday. The island looks different—more alive, more colorful—in the light of day. It's way more eclectic than Eric's island, but all the more beautiful for it. We emerge onto the beach, which is crowded with sunbathers and a group of clearly drunk college-aged kids playing beach volleyball. Day-drinking is doing nothing for their hand-eye coordination.

"Shall we walk a little and try to find someplace emptier?"

"Yes, please." We kick off our shoes and stroll along the beach with our sandals dangling from our hands and our toes sinking into the soft sand.

"This is the life." I take a deep breath of the sea air. "I should be totally freaking out right now, but I actually feel calmer than I have in a long time."

"Maybe you know you made the right decision."

"I think so." I smile at the sun, feeling the warmth on my face. I'm worried about the confession I need to make, but for now, I'm just going to enjoy this day. "I think I'm always extra at home on the beach."

"Me too," Meli agrees. "But since I grew up in Oregon, I usually spent my beach days wearing a wetsuit instead of a bikini."

"What were you like when you were a kid? Were you always interested in acting?"

We drift closer to the water until the warm waves wash over

our feet. The crowds have thinned, the groups of sunbathing tourists making way for a few local kids kicking around a ball. It's much more peaceful.

"I liked acting from a very young age, but I think that what I liked best was imagining. You know, pretending I was someone from a book or a movie."

"I did that, too. Kids made a lot of fun of me in first grade because I always spent my recesses alone on the swings, pretending that I was an adventurer named Laila flying in an airborne kayak."

"Wow, we would have really gotten along when we were kids. I spent most of first grade on the top of the play structure, overseeing my legion of frog magicians."

"Really? I thought you were always popular."

"Well, I was." Meli shrugs and stops to pick up a pink shell, which she hands to me. I fold its smooth curves into my palm. "But I went to an alternative school that was focused on imaginative play and exploration. I wasn't, like, cliché-y, cheerleader popular, but I had a couple of good friends who I did almost everything with."

"That sounds nice." Despite the similarities in our stories, I can't help feeling like Meli and I wouldn't have been friends when we were little. She's like sunshine—bright and warm. I'm not. "The only time in school I had really good friends was in fifth grade. I had this friend, Kate. We'd just moved to Colorado Springs, and she absorbed me into her friend group." Even as I talk about Kate, I'm not sure it's a wise choice.

"What happened?" Meli sounds politely curious; not like she knows the can of worms I'm on the verge of prying open.

"We moved eventually, and I had a much harder time with friends after that." It's true, although it isn't even close to the whole story. "What about your friends? What happened?"

"Some of them I'm still close with, others not so much. When we were little, it was Ryan and Tuesday and I. Eventually,

Tuesday moved to Seattle for college, fell in love, and stayed. I see her every now and then, but we aren't anywhere near as close as we used to be. Ryan and I both stayed in Portland, and now we're in a performance company together."

"Gingersnap Company, right?"

"Right." Meli looks pleased I remembered. "We started it along with two other friends who are also interested in theatre, Shin and Maria. Shin is just a fantastic actor, he makes people cry in almost every show, and he recently stepped up to direct our latest production. Maria is our stage manager and keeps our shows on the rails when we creatives get too excited. Ryan is the one who usually writes the fairy tale adaptations we use as scripts. And I do a lot of our casting and direct the more physical theatre parts."

I can't explain it, but my heart is starting to feel…strange. Empty.

"So, you have your best friend, Jen. Then you have Ryan and your other two friends with Gingersnap Company. And there's, um, Tuesday, who you don't see much but who you're still close with."

"Mm-hmm." Meli's brow wrinkles and her eyes half-close. "Hannah, you look worried. What's up?"

The usual Hannah would mumble a non-answer and try to change the subject, or maybe say nothing at all. But this is a new, braver Hannah. A Hannah who left her fiancé at the wedding because he was a jerk. I can say this.

"I'm just feeling a little…worried." I struggle to form the exact words I want to say.

"Hannah." Meli tugs me over to a dry patch of sand and sinks to the ground with her long, beautiful legs stretched out in front of her. I take a seat beside her, drawing my knees into my chest. "What's going on?"

"I'm just worried that with all those friends, you don't have room in your life…for me."

Chapter Fifteen

I want to pull Hannah into my arms. She looks so small and nervous with the wind blowing her fine hair around her face and her knees drawn up to her chest. I sit on my hands to restrain myself. My mind is full of questions of what Hannah meant when she said she was worried there wasn't room for her in my life. I'm not sure if she meant as a friend, or as something more.

"Hannah, I always have room for more friends." Because we are friends. That's all we are. And that's why I can't pull her into my arms and kiss her until her worried frown disappears.

"I don't want to be your friend." The words are firm and confident, stronger than I've heard from Hannah in most of the days I've known her. The statement sends me reeling, though.

"You don't want to be my friend?" I gesture around at the beach, the crashing cerulean waves and the soft white sand, the shouting kids and the palm trees. "That makes it a little awkward that we're stranded on a tropical island together." I'm trying to lighten the mood, but Hannah just bites her lip and tiny lines appear in her forehead.

"I…It's just…ugh."

"You don't have to explain." The phrase has gotten a little worn, but I still mean it as much as I always have.

Hannah shakes her head. "I want to explain. The words just won't come out."

"You can write—" Again, she shakes her head.

"Just…don't look at me."

"Okay." I'm nervous now. It was her idea, but maybe sharing the bed last night made her more uncomfortable than I thought. I should have insisted on sleeping on the floor. Still, it's too late now. I resolutely look at the water, guarding my heart.

"Well, I…I understand if…" Hannah mumbles. She's messing with a strand of her hair.

There's a long pause. I'm not good at waiting like this. I'm desperate to turn to Hannah and hand her a piece of paper so she can write her thoughts. I'm on the verge of asking if she wants to keep walking while she thinks. I'm not exactly impatient, but the suspense is killing me. Thankfully, she continues.

"The reason I don't like Eric"—her words are now smooth as though she's reciting from a script—"is that I don't like men at all. Or I don't think I do. I like women."

I glance at Hannah, shock and hope fighting for control of my heart. *She likes women.* The kiss conversation from the airport comes back into sharp focus. Maybe she really did want to kiss me. Hannah faces the water, and her eyes are closed. She has a strand of her golden hair wrapped around her finger and twists it as she thinks. She's beautiful.

I force myself to remain silent. In the past I might have jumped in to say that she doesn't need to tell me anything she doesn't want to or suggest that I can give her space, but I don't. I need to let her say this on her own time.

"I like *you*. When you touch me, it's…"

It's fire. Hannah doesn't need to finish. Warmth rushes through my whole body and my heart gallops double-time. This feels like a dream or a scene, not like real life. It can't be that Hannah Barnes, the world's straightest-seeming woman, is confessing romantic feelings toward me. *It can't be*. Still, I stay quiet.

"I know I'm…" She falters again, as if the momentum of

the confession is seeping away. "I'm no one's ideal…girlfriend. I *am*…awkward…and if you don't…"

Okay—screw staying silent. I take the hand that was playing with her hair into mine and squeeze it gently. She opens her eyes and glances at me, then looks at her lap as if too embarrassed to meet my gaze.

My turn. If Hannah could be brave enough to share her feelings, however scary it was, I owe her the same courtesy.

"If I had known that there was any chance of you returning my feelings, I would have asked to kiss you after brunch the first day we met." I smile as Hannah's beautiful blue eyes suddenly meet my gaze. "Since then, I've only liked you more every time we've met. You might think you're shy and awkward, but *I* think you're hilarious and intelligent and gorgeous and probably the bravest person I know."

There's a beat of silence between us while Hannah seems to take in my words. Then she shakes her head.

"Meli, you're the amazing one. You're so…" She bites her lip.

"It's all right, you can send me a list of compliments later." I flip my hair over my shoulder to punctuate the joke, and Hannah laughs. Then I'm laughing, too, and the tension of the moment is broken.

"No, no," Hannah finally says, clutching her stomach. I regain my breath and the laughter fades away. "But you're basically my favorite person. I mean, no, that's too far. Oh—"

I wave my hand before she can get too hung up on her compliment, even as my heart beats in my chest harder than I thought was possible.

"You know, you're basically my favorite person, too." I'm not just saying it to make her feel better. It's true. I've never met anyone like Hannah, and I doubt I ever will again.

"Really?" Hannah presses a hand to her heart like she's the recipient of a fantastic prize. "Thank you. And—sorry. I meant to do this better. I was thinking we could stand on a cliff at sunset or something." She blushes.

"This is pretty perfect." I gesture again at the waves and the sand, hardly noticing them. My attention is completely focused on the woman beside me. My lips are tingly and my heart aches to pull her into my arms and kiss her, finally. I'm trying to figure out how to bring this up in a chill, no-pressure way, when Hannah shifts so that she's kneeling. I rise onto my knees, too, and suddenly, we are just a few inches apart.

"In the airport, I was trying, in a roundabout way, to ask you to kiss me." Hannah's voice is low and soft. It tugs at something deep inside me.

"You were? I wondered, but I couldn't believe it. Do…" My heart hammers in my chest. "Do you want to kiss me now?"

She nods. "Do you?"

It's all I can do not to laugh. She's offering me the thing I've been dreaming of for the last few weeks. Her need to double-check if I want it is both sexy and sweet.

"Of course."

And yet, as Hannah slowly leans closer, I have a rush of nerves. I don't really know that much about her dating history, but I'm pretty sure this will be her first kiss with a woman. If it doesn't go well, I may sabotage not only any chance at a relationship between Hannah, but also her whole potential lesbian future.

Then Hannah's lips are on mine, and all rational and irrational thoughts float away like a fluffy cloud in a blue sky. At first, we exchange a few chaste kisses, our lips barely touching as I rest my hand on Hannah's waist. I mean to stop there to give Hannah a chance to process, but Hannah has no such plans. She leans in even closer, opening her mouth with the softest of sighs. Suddenly, we're kissing deeply, and I realize we're pressed together with our arms around each other. She feels soft and warm and wonderful against me and it's all I can do not to lay us both down on the sand and explore what else I can do to make her moan and sigh.

But we're on a public beach. A beach with children.

Hannah seems to realize this at the same moment as I do, because we both pull away—with great effort on my part—and sit back on our heels. Hannah's fair cheeks are flushed pink, her lips are still slightly parted, and her eyes are wide.

"So, how was that?" I feel like I'm surveying my audience after a performance, and the thought makes me smile.

"I liked that." Hannah smiles almost giddily. Her eyes are extra wide. "I knew it!"

The corners of my mouth tug up. "You knew it?"

"Well." Hannah blushes even deeper. "Remember when you helped me zip my dress?"

"Remember?" I laugh a little. "That memory is pretty much imprinted on my brain. I was so worried I'd freaked you out."

"You didn't…but when you touched my back, I got all these…shivers. And that's when I thought, maybe kisses were supposed to be more than okay. With Eric, they were okay. But with you—"

"More than okay." I reach over my shoulder to pat myself on the back. "Good job, Meli." Underneath the jokes, I'm practically glowing. If I could stay here on this beach forever, kissing Hannah and hearing her explain how she was attracted to me for way longer than I would have ever guessed, I would.

Just then, the soccer ball comes bouncing between us.

"Hey!" One of the kids yells in accented English and waves. "Ball, please!"

Hannah pushes herself to her feet and gives the ball a good hard kick, sending it soaring back to the kids.

"Thanks!"

"No problem!"

I blink at her.

"Did you just talk to that kid on purpose?"

"Yeah." Hannah shrugs. "Kids are different. I can always talk to kids."

"Aren't you just full of surprises?" I get to my feet, too, brushing the sand off my shorts. "Shall we keep walking? You can tell me more good things about me."

"Oh, sure." We both turn toward the direction we haven't seen yet. Hannah slips her hand into mine and squeezes. Then she gives me a shy smile as if asking if this is okay, and I squeeze back.

Hand in hand, we walk down the beach again, exchanging compliments and laughing at nothing. It feels like we've always walked this way. It's magical. I don't think I've ever been happier.

CHAPTER SIXTEEN

The day unfurls beautifully. We walk along the beach for another hour or so, talking about nothing in particular. Meli's hand feels so right in mine, like I've only just found a missing piece of me. I can't believe it took me so long to say something, so long to be sure.

"So," Meli says. "Am I ever going to hear that cookie story?"

"Oh, sure. Although it's more embarrassing now that we know each other better. Okay, so, I was at this big orientation that I told you about, and there was a plate of cookies in the middle. I reached for one and took a big bite, but just then, the meeting started. I felt like I was crunching so loudly!" I shake my head.

Instead of replying, Meli just stares at me. Then she bursts into laughter. "*That's* the cookie story? After all this build-up, it's just about you crunching loudly?"

"It was in an important meeting!" I protest.

"I know, I know, but my story is about eating sticks of butter and yours is about something that happens to people on more or less a daily basis."

I cross my arms, pulling my hand from hers, and stick my lip out in a mock pout. "I happen to like my cookie story."

Meli puts an arm around my waist. "If you like it, then I

like it, too. The cookie story is my new favorite story of all. I'm totally going to get Gingersnap Company to make it into a play."

"It should probably be a musical." I put my arm around her, too. "And there should be at least three different kinds of trees in it."

"Oh, obviously. And that animator of yours can make the movie version. What was his name?"

"Miyazaki."

"Yes. Miyazaki can make the movie."

We lean into each other and walk on, trading increasingly outrageous ideas for what should appear in the *Cookie Movie-Slash-Musical.*

Just as Meli and I are talking about how we're starting to get hungry, we also realize we are on the stretch of beach with even fewer tourists. Near the edge of the beach is a stand selling fresh corn on the cob, fried bread with savory fillings, and hot cones of French fries. Meli buys us a couple of each offering and we sit on the sand, listening to music playing on an old radio, and eating until our stomachs are full to bursting. The music has a great beat we both sway to, our shoulders brushing. It sounds somehow familiar, even though I've never heard this particular tune before.

Meli wads up the paper wrapper of her fried bread, tosses it expertly into our paper bag, and falls gracefully back on the sand. I have an urge to climb on top of her, maybe run my hand along her stomach. *Wow.* I've never had feelings this intense. Instead of acting on my urge, I flop onto my back next to her and we both gaze up at the opalescent blue of the sky. I watch a few puffy clouds float across the expanse.

"This is the life," I sigh. "I don't want to go back to Portland."

"Really?" Meli rolls onto her side and props herself up to look at me. "Are you worried about running into Eric?"

"I mean, yes, but I don't think we really run in the same circles. I just don't want to go back to work and real life. Do you?"

"Sure. Work isn't fun all the time, but I love performing and I love working with my kids."

"I wish I felt that way about copywriting, but honestly, it's a little boring. Especially since it's just marketing materials for a company that makes tools. There're only so many ways to discuss how versatile a drill is, you know?"

"Is there something you'd like to do instead?"

"I don't know." I reach my hands up to make a pillow behind my head and wiggle to get more comfortable. The sand is warm beneath me. "I kind of feel like everything is up in the air. I think Eric was expecting me to quit my job once we got married—well, I know he was. He told me."

"He did?" Meli wrinkles her eyebrows. "Did *you* want to quit your job?"

"Yeah, kind of. But not to become his arm candy. He phrased it like he didn't want me to overtax myself when I didn't make much money anyway."

"I'm really glad you left him. Not just because leaving him made space for us to be a couple."

"Yeah..." I struggle to pull together how I want to respond, and Meli gives me a concerned look.

"I'm sorry, is it too soon?"

I shake my head. "It's just...you...we..."

"That I said we're a couple?" Meli fills in. She drops her gaze. "I'm sorry. I know we just kissed once and it's way too early to be throwing those kinds of phrases around. Just ignore it."

"Chill."

Meli looks surprised for a moment, just like I feel, before she bursts out laughing. It's short-lived, though, and she's quickly back to looking at me with those intense brown eyes.

I wish I could just kiss her instead of trying to stumble my way through what I need to say, but it's important. I look past her, up at the blue of the sky, and try to talk like I'm alone and no one is listening.

"I would like to…be a…couple. With you." I sneak a glance at Meli and see that she's grinning.

"Great, then, girlfriend."

"And…about the kissing?" I can see Meli's eyes dim, and I quickly press on. "Can we…do that more?"

Meli smiles again. She bends her head to mine and plants one quick kiss on my lips.

"We should probably save most of the kissing for our room, though."

The thought of *our room* makes my heart race with excitement and nerves. I know I want to explore this newfound connection. I'm also worried. I've never…slept with anyone. I could be bad at it. I could be so bad at it that Meli decides I'm too much work to bother.

"What are you worrying about now?" Meli smooths her thumb over the circle between my eyebrows. "You're all frowny."

"I'm worried about…you know. Sleeping together."

"Oh. Right. Well, we don't have to."

Now I'm alarmed.

"No, I want to! If, I mean, you…" I reach to cover my face, but Meli takes my hand before I can.

"Of course I want to sleep with you. When and if that's what *you* want." Her voice is amazingly sexy. There's a flutter of something deep inside me, and heat pools between my legs. *Is that normal?*

"But I never…I never slept with anyone. I might not be very good."

"Well," Meli's voice is still low and soft and deep, "the most important thing about sex for me is that the people involved enjoy it and care about each other. I think we can swing that, don't you?"

I nod. I'm very warm now. It's like someone turned up the temperature of the sun. Meli flops onto her back again, ending the moment of intensity. It's a relief when she changes the topic.

"Anyway, sorry. I got distracted. We were talking about your job. Is there something you think you'd like to do better?"

I shrug. "I don't know. I think doing the same thing for eight hours every day is kind of rough, no matter what your job is."

"I get that. That's why I like my job. I'm always doing different things—an hour of this rehearsal, teaching that class, then a performance. There's a lot of variety."

"I like baking." I'm not sure why I've said that—it's not like I've ever baked professionally. "I mean, I always thought it would be fun to be a baker. They wake up early, spend some hours in a nice-smelling kitchen without talking to many people, and then go home."

"So, why don't you look into baking when we get back to Portland? Maybe you could do some freelance copywriting, instead of working a specific job, bake a few days a week, and add on something else if it interests you."

"I don't know." I let out a short sigh. "Freelancing does seem like a good fit, since I could communicate with a lot of clients online. And I do like the idea of trying baking, though I would need to learn a lot about it first. It all seems like a really big step. Although, the time when I stopped following other people's expectations is the time I started being the happiest."

"The time as in…yesterday?" I laugh a little.

"Yeah, but for the last couple of weeks, really. Since I met you." I touch Meli's hand. "I think I started taking small steps out of the ordinary, like agreeing to meet you at Burgerville and not flying here with Eric and really talking to my brother until I got to the point where I could just walk away from my own wedding. Speaking of which, maybe I should check my phone. I want to know what happened with my family."

I pull my phone from my pocket and, yes, it's lit up with a dozen messages. There's nothing from Eric, which is a relief. A few messages from my parents share sentiments like *Get back here right now* and *We're so disappointed in you*. Okay, so they've noticed I'm missing, at least. There's one message from Brad.

I'm proud of you. Call me when you're ready.

It warms my heart, and I show it to Meli, who has found her own phone.

"Aww, that's great. It sounds like he's in your corner."

I reply to my brother right away and ask how everything is, and that's that. The benefit of not knowing a lot of people is that there aren't a lot of people to explain yourself to when you become a runaway bride.

"I got a couple messages from Jen," Meli says, tilting her phone toward me. "It's, uh…do you want to see?"

"Yeah, all right." I take the phone from her and scroll through the messages from Jen. I am more than a little nervous.

*Let me know how it goes with Hannah! *heart emoji* *two girls kissing emoji**

"Oh!" Meli sees the message I'm reading and claps her hands over her face, moaning a little. "I went too far back in the chat, Hannah. Sorry."

"Jen knows you like me?"

"Well, yeah. Honestly, I kind of couldn't shut up about you."

"Really?" My cheeks are warm again. I'm not sure I've blushed this much in my life. "That's sweet."

Meli grins. "I'm glad you think so. Okay, scroll down. Oh, but you might want to skip the message about your brother."

It's too late for the warning.

*Brad and I banged *red lips emoji**

"It's okay, that could have been much more graphic. I definitely saw this coming, even if I'd rather not have had it confirmed." I keep scrolling. I'm used to my brother's active dating life by now, so I'm not too affected by this—even though things do seem more serious with Jen than with the women he's been with before.

Nothing this morning about your disappearance. You better update me soon!

*We had the dolphin swim this morning. It was awful. Those poor dolphins are kept in a little aquarium. Can you imagine? I think it's illegal. *angry face emoji**

"Those poor dolphins." I shake my head. "Maybe we can report him to PETA."

"Let's add it to the to-do list."

Still no updates on your disappearance, but Crystal was sitting next to Eric at lunch.

Meli rolls back to her side. "How do you feel about the Crystal thing?" She looks at me with concern and I laugh.

"Meli, I can't stress this enough. I don't love him. I never loved him. In retrospect, I'm not even sure I *liked* him all that much—especially since meeting you. I never should have let all this get so far. I like *you*. I would be sad if *you* were dating someone else. Him dating Crystal—or whatever he's doing with her—is kind of a relief."

"Even so, it was your wedding."

"Honestly, I think I'm the one at fault here. I'm the runaway bride in this scenario. If he wants to dress Crystal up as me and tell everyone that she's Hannah Barnes, I'm okay with that. Maybe she can do all my public speaking for me."

Meli laughs. "Okay, okay. I'll stop. But if you do feel upset about any of this, you can talk to me."

"I know. I can almost always get myself to talk to you. Except when it's really important, and then I get all…" I shrug and she laughs again. I like that she knows what I mean without me having to put it in perfect words. We lie there for a while longer, sifting sand through our fingers, and watching the clouds pass overhead. We don't talk much, but Meli just being next to me is more than enough.

I finally feel at peace, not only with another person, but with myself. I'm being brave, or at least my version of brave, and standing up for what I want and what I believe in. Best of all, that bravery has led to a chance for real happiness with Meli. I don't think I've ever been happier.

Chapter Seventeen

When we return to the hotel room, it is already dark. The day flew by and I'm surprised it's already so late.

After our return journey along the beach, we changed into our swimsuits, rented snorkel gear, and took a long, splashy dip in the ocean. We dived to look at coral and fish and even saw one beautiful green turtle that moved with a certain kind of mesmerizing grace. We stopped for dinner at a Mexican restaurant in town, where we feasted on tacos and chips with guacamole. After that was another stroll and ice cream. It was just about the best first date ever, if that's what it was. And I definitely think it was.

And now here we are, in the doorway of our room, again facing the prospect of one small bed to share. Except now we're a brand-new couple instead of just friends. I glance at Hannah and see that she's messing with her hands again, sliding her fingers up and down each other and pressing her nails. I recognize it as a sign of anxiety. I quickly take her hands in mine.

"There's no pressure, okay?" I tug on her hands gently until she looks up at me. "I can even sleep on the floor."

She looks alarmed and shakes her head so fast that her hair whips around her face.

"*No!* Sleep on the bed. *Please.*"

"How could I turn down an invitation like that?" I wink at her, and she looks slightly more relaxed.

I am glad Hannah has been so adamant we share a bed and so quick to hold my hand. Hannah struggles a lot to express her feelings, but she seems sure about me, based on what she said earlier on the beach. Even if she's nervous about some parts of our newfound relationship.

"You can't." She smiles at me, then reaches up to run her hand through my hair. A small shower of sand comes away with her fingers. "I was about to compliment your hair, which I've always liked, but maybe we need showers first."

"I think you might be right." I shake my head ruefully. "Want to shower first?" She tugs her hair, causing another cascade of sand, and nods sheepishly.

Half an hour later, we both sit on the bed. We have our legs under the covers and are propped against the wall with the pillow at our backs. This moment reminds me more of a sleepover than a date, but I'm not complaining. Any time with Hannah is well spent.

"Can I ask you something?" Hannah's voice is soft.

"Sure."

"How did you know you liked women?"

"Ah. Right…I knew pretty early, mostly because my parents were super open about all the kinds of families and relationships that are out there." I smile at the memory. "When I was six, I wrote a story for school about my best friend at the time, Meredith. In the story, she and I were living in a house together and raising our children."

"Should I be worried about this Meredith?" Hannah furrows her eyebrows in mock concern.

"You're good, she's married and expecting her first child now. Plus, she's grown up to be a bit religious for my taste—not that there's anything wrong with that. But I'd prefer you any day." I shift a little, smoothing the blanket over our legs. "What about you?"

I'm expecting her to tell me that she only just realized that she's a lesbian, possibly because of me. A lot of people only realize who they are later in life. Perhaps this is true more often if they grew up in religious or conservative families like Hannah's. I'm wrong, though.

"Well, remember that friend, Kate? I kind of…had a crush on her. I mean, I didn't really get that it was a crush at the time, but I knew I wanted to be close to her." She pauses and bites her lip. "I thought she felt the same way. I…I kissed her on the cheek at a sleepover and it was a complete disaster. She freaked out, my parents freaked out, and I locked that part of me away for a long time. I figured it was better to make everyone else happy than to be happy myself. I wasn't even sure that things would be different with a woman. I mean, kissing him wasn't all that special, so how was I supposed to know if it would be better with a woman? It didn't seem worth the risk to explore my feelings more. Then…well, I met you."

Wow. This is even better than what I was expecting. My heart is full, and I reach out to Hannah. She snuggles into my side. It's nice, but a little uncomfortable, so we wiggle down and around until we're lying on our sides, facing each other. Her soft blue eyes are only inches from mine. As are those pink lips.

"I'm glad it was me who you decided to take a chance on," I whisper. Up close, she's even more beautiful than I had noticed before—or maybe it's just that I have the chance to stare now without being creepy. Her blue eyes have little green flecks in them, and she has a sprinkling of freckles across her cheeks. Her nose turns up slightly at the end in a way I find absolutely adorable. I want to kiss it. So I do.

Hannah's eyes widen and she laughs.

"You kissed my nose!" The statement, so full of surprise and happiness, makes me laugh, too.

"Is that okay?"

"Of course." She snuggles closer. "So, tell me, who was in your life between Meredith and me?"

"You want to hear about my exes?" I wrinkle my nose and she quickly plants a kiss on it, then retreats.

"You don't have to tell me. But I'm curious. I'll start. There was the disastrous incident with Kate. I went on one date with my friend's boyfriend's friend in college and left after forty-five minutes because he made fun of me for having trouble speaking. Then there was Eric, which you know about, and now you." She smiles.

"I like the sound of that last one. She sounds sexy."

"She is."

Okay, I felt that compliment. I quickly brush past it to keep myself from sliding a hand under Hannah's pajama shirt and seeing if I can get her to say that again, maybe using the actual word.

"Well, my dating history isn't that exciting. I went out with a girl in high school for a little while, but mostly because we were the only two lesbians and it seemed like the thing to do. Neither of us were that into each other. Then in college, I dated Kami for a year. We were good together, but we wanted different things. Since then"—I wince—"I've had a couple of flings, maybe more than a couple, but nothing serious." I worry what Hannah will think of me.

Hannah appears to take my story in stride, although she still has questions. "Why didn't you find anything serious?"

"It wasn't that I wasn't looking," I say. "Although, I wasn't looking seriously, either. It's just that nothing felt quite right for the long term. My friends like to tease me for being too picky, but I've always known what I wanted, and I didn't want to settle. Plus, I'll admit it was fun to explore what's out there." I might as well be honest with her about my history from the beginning.

"What is it that you want?"

"A real connection. A spark. Someone I can laugh with and grow with and rely on. Someone who gets my sense of humor and who is willing to be both playful and serious. Someone like you." Hannah smiles at this, but I'm not done. "And, well, someone who wants kids. Not right now, but eventually. That's important to me. It's why Kami and I broke up."

Hannah nods. "I want kids, too…I always thought I'd like to have a lot."

I squeeze her closer. "Me too."

"Really?" She looks excited. "Eric said maybe one or two, which wasn't my preference, but I had compromised on so much already, it was easy to give in again. How many do you want?"

"It depends, of course, but I always thought four or five would be kind of perfect."

"Me too!"

"Of course," I add quickly, realizing how the conversation might sound, "I don't mean I want to have kids right this moment, or even that you're the person I'll have them with. No pressure."

"Okay." Hannah laughs softly in the dark. "Let's just assume there's no pressure from either of us, okay?" Once again, she surprises me with how chill she is about certain parts of our relationship. There's no guile there, and she seems either unaware of or uninterested in playing games.

"That seems fair. So, how about you? I told you my type, what's yours?"

Hannah shifts a little. I can't see her face well in the dark, but I think she's a bit uncomfortable.

"I don't know. I hadn't thought about it much."

"Let me guess, you like half-French, half-Indian actors with curly hair and a great sense of humor?" I make a funny face to show that I'm teasing, though she probably can't see it in the dark.

"Hmm, true. Maybe I also have a very specific type." There's a pause. "I guess I like people who accept me for who I am, who make me laugh, and who like adventures. And someone I connect with, like you said. Someone like you."

Then she kisses me. Her lips are warm and soft. It makes me ache for more, but I hold back. I expect that, with all her difficulties talking and telling people what she wants, Hannah will be reserved about going any further and it will take time for her to want more. I'm okay with that. There's a lot to be said about just kissing, especially when it's as charged as ours. I want to give Hannah what she wants, whatever she wants.

I'm wrong again. After about two minutes of rather chaste kissing, Hannah slips her hand under my pajama top. I must gasp because she pulls her hand back like she's been burned.

"Sorry!"

"No, no." I take her hand and kiss it. "I just wasn't expecting that."

"But it was okay?"

"Yes."

I kiss her again, and she slides her hand under my shirt once more, brushing up the length of my spine. The gesture makes me shiver and lean into her. Slowly, cautiously, I slip my hand under her shirt, sliding my fingers up until I brush the soft skin under her breast. Hannah sighs quietly, so I run my thumb over her nipple.

For someone who struggles to speak, Hannah hardly struggles to communicate with her body. In moments our pajamas are flung on the floor and we're exploring each other. It's the best sex I've ever had. Hannah isn't particularly skilled, but her enthusiasm and her soft moans of pleasure more than make up for it.

Afterward, when we're lying in each other's arms and I'm just starting to doze, Hannah nudges me. Her eyes are shining.

"Did you know sex could be that good?" She pauses, a flicker of uncertainty crossing her face. "I mean, it was good for me. But I didn't really know what I was doing. Was I okay?"

I draw her lips to mine and kiss her hard. My heart is so, so full.

"Hannah, you were wonderful. That was amazing. And no. I didn't know it could be that good. And you know why it was? Because of how we feel about each other. It's like I said on the beach. Sex is the best when both people care about each other." I want to say it's because we love each other, but we haven't said those words yet, and now doesn't feel like the time. I don't want her to think I'm only confessing my love because I'm still on a high from the sex.

I'm telling the truth when I say it was amazing. There was something earth-shattering about sex with Hannah. I replay bits of our last few hours together in my mind, and every time it fills me with warmth.

We talk a bit more, but we're both very tired, and before long my eyelids are heavy.

Chapter Eighteen

I wake in Meli's arms with one of my legs slid between hers and her arm flung across my waist. The same as yesterday, and yet different. Contentment washes through me as I reflect on our time and conversation. We slept together last night. I didn't know what to expect, but I wasn't expecting anything as wonderful as what happened. It was neither as straightforward as the movies nor as awkward as overheard conversations about other people's first times. Yes, it had been romantic and very sexy—but we'd laughed, too. I want to do it again, preferably as soon as possible.

I just hope Meli feels the same way. There's probably a lot of room for improvement on my part.

"Hey." Meli stirs slightly and nestles closer. "Are you awake?"

"No, you're dreaming."

She smiles against my neck. "I believe it."

I've never been one to laze around after waking up, but I'm starting to see the benefits, especially when she kisses me again. The kisses turn more passionate, and pretty soon we're pressed together with a growing need.

"Do you want to have a repeat of last night?" Meli's voice is low and filled with desire. Her voice heightens the warmth that's already spreading through me and pooling between my legs.

"Yes, please."

❖

We finally roll ourselves out of bed, take turns in the bathroom, and get dressed, this time agreeing to start the day with swimsuits under our clothes. The whole time, we exchange charged glances that make it difficult to leave the room instead of falling back into bed. Despite the difficulty, we manage to make it out of the room with little more than a quick kiss. Downstairs, Laurence offers us more cocoa tea, fruits, and pastries.

"There's a bigger room available starting tonight." He slides the plate of fruit onto our table. "If you're planning to stay in town, I could move you there." Meli looks quickly to me, but I grin and shake my head. I like our small room and our small bed. She grins back.

"It's all right, we're on a bit of a budget, so I think we'll stick to the small room," Meli says. Laurence nods at her and politely pardons himself to go introduce a few new guests to the concept of cocoa tea.

"So, what shall we do today?" I lean back in my chair and cross one leg over the other. I feel an easy, relaxed calm that I've never felt before. I'm not sure if it's sex in general or if this happiness comes from sex with Meli, but either way, I like it. I hope I'll always feel this wonderful after sex with Meli.

"We can explore the island more," Meli suggests. "I'd love another dip in the water."

"Ooh, let's go to the beach on the far side where people see turtles."

"And then maybe, later, we could…" Meli's gaze intensifies as she bites her lip slightly. "We could spend a little more time in our room."

"I like that idea." We grin at each other like fools for several minutes, then turn our attention to the food. The fruit is as delicious as it was yesterday, and we finally sample the pastries. We joke about how we need the carbs for endurance. They aren't bad, but we agree the fruit is still the star of the meal.

After breakfast, we set off toward the beach. As we walk, Meli and I tangle our fingers together as naturally as if we've done so every day for our whole lives.

"I think we should buy snorkels instead of renting them today," Meli suggests. "I doubt this will be our last swim of the trip."

So, we stop by a cute little dive shop. Inside, I gravitate toward the wall of water toys.

"There's an inflatable dolphin." I point to the wall display. "And a turtle!"

"Do you want one?" Meli raises her eyebrows as we walk closer to the merchandise. I flush. I am a full-grown adult admiring children's water toys.

"No…" Despite all we've shared, I am still embarrassed to admit I would love to ride around on the broad back of that turtle.

"Oh, that's too bad." Meli rests a hand on the inflatable turtle box. "Because I thought it would be fun to get one. They're only, like, ten bucks in US dollars."

"Really?" I'm not a hundred percent sure that she's not teasing me.

"*Really*, really. So, turtle, dolphin, or jellyfish?"

"I have to go with the turtle." We grab the box, along with a pair of snorkeling masks, and make a beeline for the check-out counter. Then we carry our purchases to the beach and dump them in a pile on the sand.

"Okay." Meli slides open the turtle box. "Let's get this show on the road." She unfurls the length of plastic that will soon be our aquatic friend and blows experimentally into the inflation tube. Nothing happens. She tries a bigger breath. Still nothing.

"Want me to try?"

She passes the turtle over and, with a few quick puffs, I manage to inflate approximately one eighth of a percent of the turtle's body. We make eye contact and giggle.

"This may take a while," I say. "I wonder how kids are supposed to do this." We pass the toy back and forth. At first, I try to ignore the fact that our mouths are basically touching, but I don't have to ignore anything about *us*, anymore. I grin happily through my efforts for several minutes.

With the turtle finally inflated, we grab our snorkels and masks, strip to our swimsuits, and head for the water. The turtle is balanced between us. As soon as we splash into the water, we drop the turtle and I leap onto it, gliding across the surface until a wave catches me and pushes me back to Meli's feet. She looks at me with a small smile and an eyebrow arched over her eye.

"How do you feel that went?"

"Perfectly." I try to appear dignified while lying on an inflated plastic turtle. "Thanks for asking." I stand and we push the turtle out into deeper water, where we both put our elbows on the turtle's back while we put our masks on. I then climb aboard the turtle for a quick survey of the beach we left behind.

Suddenly, Meli flips the turtle, which sends me splashing into the water. I come up a moment later, not much worse for the wear since I already had my mask on, to find her sitting atop the turtle's back, posture as straight and regal as a queen's.

"This," she proclaims, "is my turtle."

I gape at her.

"What makes you think that? Tory is clearly mine." To prove my point, I grab her by the leg and pull her into the water, then flop my belly onto the turtle and swing one leg over. Meli comes up laughing.

"Tory?"

"It's a great name!"

"Sure." We spend a few minutes in battle over ownership of Tory, pushing each other into the water and clambering on top. I haven't had this much fun in...I'm not sure how long. Finally, we reach an impasse, mainly because we're both out of breath. I flop my upper body onto Tory's back and Meli joins me, her head only inches from mine. Her hair is soaking wet, which has made it even more unruly than usual, and she's grinning broadly.

"That was so cool! I haven't played King of the Raft since I was a kid."

"It was fun," I say. "As long as we can agree that, in the end, *I* am the king of the turtle."

"Whatever you say, love." Meli presses a quick and salty kiss to my lips, then slides headfirst off the turtle with a delicate splash.

I'm left on Tory's back, pressing a hand to my tingling lips like a schoolgirl and wondering what Meli meant when she called me *love*. I don't have long to wonder, though, before Meli grabs one of my feet and pulls me into the water with her. We tread water together, just a few inches apart.

"What was that about?" I protest. "I thought we agreed I won."

"We did, but I saw a real turtle and I wanted to show you. Come on!" Meli dives under and I follow. The whole world goes quiet with the press of water as I release my snorkel, relying on my mask. The ocean here is almost crystal clear, giving me a perfect view of the coral reef and its inhabitant fish below. Beside me, Meli swims down, her bare slender legs kicking and arms pulling. I take a moment to wonder at her, this woman who's so much more fascinating than even the best marine life. She looks like a mermaid with her hair floating around her head and her brown eyes bright and sparkling beneath her mask. We kick down, barefoot, and the coral reef rises until it's much closer than the surface. I spot coral formations and a school of colorful fish darting back and forth. Seaweed sways in the current, offering hiding places for larger fish and the outline of a creature I suspect is an eel, though I can't get close enough to confirm before I run out of breath.

I kick back to the surface. Meli comes up for a breath a moment after me, then we dive together.

Meli waves at me and points. When I follow her gesture, I spot the small green turtle. It paddles along in a surprisingly elegant way. Its small flippers propel it up to the surface for a breath. I watch it until my lungs start to burn, then follow it at a distance to the surface with Meli at my side.

"Wow! A turtle!" I am slightly breathless. "They're my favorite."

"I know!" She beams at me. "This might be the best day I've ever had."

"I have to agree." I bob beside her, thoughtful now. "I was dreading today."

"Right…It was supposed to be your wedding day."

"Thank goodness it isn't. I do wonder what everyone's doing over on Saint Sofia, though."

"Petting captive dolphins?" Meli suggests. "Holding conferences to decide who's the biggest jerk?"

I laugh, then cough a little on inhaled water. "Probably. I'm just glad that I'm not there. I don't think they have inflatable turtles. Shall we dive more?"

So, Meli and I dive again, pushing through the clear water. I swim as deep as I can on one breath and find myself surrounded for a few heartbeats by a school of silvery fish swimming in unison. On the next dive, I follow a shiny blue fish with a box-shaped face toward the horizon. On the next, Meli and I go down together, hand in hand, and share an underwater kiss. A little water gets in my mouth, but it's worth it.

Back on the surface, I spot Tory floating away and swim furiously after him, kicking up huge splashes of white water with my legs, before grabbing him by one leg and towing him back toward Meli. We're both a bit tired after that and we paddle lazily toward shore. When we get out, we both lie on the wet sand for a few minutes, water washing over our legs, Tory between us.

"I love swimming," she says with a happy sigh. "That's the one thing I don't like about Portland. We don't have enough swimmable outdoor water."

"I mean, you can technically swim in the Willamette. People do."

"Yeah, but it's just such an off-putting color and so cold. Nothing like this."

After a few minutes of companionable silence, I peel myself from the sand and head toward our pile of clothes, ready to dry off and dress for lunch.

Except our clothes are gone.

I look around the sand, alarmed.

"Meli?" She jogs to me. "Is it just me, or are our clothes gone?"

"Looking for these?" Like a villain in an animated movie, a tourist in a baseball cap turns slowly toward us. My dress and Meli's shorts, along with our phones, dangle from his hands. My heart stops when I see his face. *Oh no.*

It's Eric.

Of course it is.

"How did you find us?" My tone is pleasantly cold and clear. Usually, I might stammer or just be silent, but today I'm firm. Eric should *not* mess with me and Meli.

"It wasn't that hard. A buddy of mine tracked your phone." Eric holds the offending piece of technology between two fingers. His face looks as disgusted as if he held a rat.

"Great. Well, give it back." I feel like a little kid on a

school playground watching a bully take her lunch money. Yet my voice hasn't failed me.

The phalanx of Eric's four jerky groomsmen stand from where they were sitting on the sand. It's scary and intimidating, but I also wonder how long they spent practicing this while we were in the water. I clasp my hands over my stomach. I wish I wasn't in a wet swimsuit for this interaction.

Still, I can do this.

"I don't think so. Look, our wedding is scheduled for sunset. It's time to come back."

I shake my head.

"No."

Meli slips her hand into mine. It's a comfort. Eric sees this and sneers like a thirteen-year-old boy cracking an inappropriate joke.

"So, *Milly* is why you think you're a lesbian."

I squeeze Meli's hand, partially to offer comfort, partially to be comforted. And partially to confirm that I don't *think* anything. I *know* I'm a lesbian.

"I…you…" *Oh no. Why are words failing me now?* Well, I know why. It's because I'm standing here, in a swimsuit, facing down my ex-fiancé and his hoard of goons. I'd be nervous enough talking to any group this large, much less one made up of such unfriendly faces.

"I…uh…" Hunter mimics me. They all reek of alcohol. Meli tenses beside me as Eric and the other groomsmen laugh.

"Don't talk to her like that," Meli snaps. I'm torn between feeling happy she's standing up for me—again—and guilty I'm the kind of person who needs to be stood up for. I should be defending myself against these jerks. My knees tremble.

"Or what, you'll fight us?" Eric laughs. "Yeah, right. Good one. Hannah, come on. Enough of this. I waited patiently for you to get over this little hiccup, but if you don't marry me, it could be disastrous for my company. I can't have people thinking I was left at the altar. This marriage is the only way for people, including your family, to respect you or me. Can you try being a little less self-absorbed for once?"

"You…" *Ugh!* I want to shout at him that there's no possible way I'm going to marry him, not only because I love Meli but also because he's the world's biggest jerk, but I can't seem to form the sentence out loud.

"And you, Milly." Eric shakes his head at my girlfriend. "What are you thinking? I know Hannah seems like an easy target, but that doesn't mean that you can try to lure her away. I put a lot of effort into making her an acceptable wife."

"Well." Meli looks from me to the group of guys. Her voice is cold. "This has been fun, but we have places to be. Give back our clothes and phones and we'll be on our way."

"Yeah, right." Eric chuckles again. I did not notice how sinister he was while we were dating. His real personality is very disturbing and reflects poorly on my choice in men. And it reflects even more poorly on him. "Boys, let's do this."

This starts with Eric grabbing me by the upper arm and trying to tug me after him. His grip is hard enough to bruise. Hunter grabs Meli at the same time. Their genius plan apparently involves dragging two unwilling women through the streets of a tourist town and onto the ferry. Once they get us back to the wedding, their delusion probably includes putting me in a dress and getting me to recite some vows.

Or, more likely, they didn't think this through at all. I bet that jerk thought I would come back willingly when he came to fetch me. I haven't objected before when I've been pushed into situations I didn't want to be in.

Unfortunately for them, they've made a key misjudgment about me. They think I won't stand up for myself, which is true—when it comes to words. I'm much more a woman of action, and this social situation has a very clear set of rules.

I deliver a swift kick between Eric's legs, making him

squeal and keel over on the sand, clutching himself. I'm tempted to send another kick into his ribs, but I don't think that would be appropriate even for this social situation. I don't want to become a bully. Instead, I pick up the clothes and phone he dropped and bend low over his face. He looks up at me, eyes wide.

"You bitch," he hisses. "I could have given you everything. No one will ever love you. Least of all your family!"

I take a moment to gather myself and solidify what I want to say. "Her name," my words are careful and measured, "is Meli."

I stand tall and turn to the groomsmen. Hunter has let go of Meli and is rubbing the side of his face, which is now bright red against the rest of his pale skin. Meli is rubbing one of her hands. She looks surprised. The groomsmen look at me, probably expecting me to say something. *Oh no.*

"You…you better leave. Or I'll kick you, too." They all look sufficiently frightened, which is satisfying. I wish I could give them a proper lecture on respecting women and making better life choices, but this will have to do for now.

I hold out my hand to Meli, and she knits her fingers between mine.

"What she said." Meli nods at me. Together, we stride away from the beach. I am trying not to run. A few passersby give us strange looks, but I don't care. I feel like Harry Potter at the end of a school year, villains defeated, head held high.

As soon as we step onto a side street, though, I burst into tears. I'm a little surprised. I thought I handled myself well, all things considered, but I must have been more stressed than I realized. Meli gathers me into her arms.

"Are you okay?"

I nod, pressing my face into her hair. "I didn't know what to say."

"Oh, love." Meli pulls back, looks into my eyes, and wipes

my tears with her thumbs. "You did great. I was so impressed with that kick."

"He wasn't right, was he?" I manage to ask. "About me?"

"About you what? That you were being unreasonable? No. That your family won't love you anymore? I'd say the love your parents show you isn't purehearted now, but your brother seems great."

"No. I mean about no one ever…loving me."

It's my biggest fear. I know I'm shy, awkward, and not that pretty. I know I'm not girly enough or successful enough. And I know that when I try to express myself, it's more likely to come out as stutters and misplaced words than coherent thoughts. I can't even order properly in a restaurant, for goodness' sake. But I still hope one person can see past my faults and love me for who I am—because despite my shyness, I am pretty special, and I deserve that kind of love. Just like everyone else.

"Hannah." Meli takes both of my hands in hers and presses her forehead to mine. "Listen to me."

"Hannah! Meli!"

I hear Meli groan softly.

We break apart to see Jen tearing toward us on the narrow street. She's wearing a hideous pink dress with puffy sleeves. Brad is in hot pursuit, his hair tousled, in a suit and matching tie. They stop in front of us, breathing hard.

"Watch…out," Jen pants. "Eric…and groomsmen…"

"Yeah, we saw them. Thanks." Meli doesn't look quite as excited to see her friend as I would have guessed she would be. And she isn't making eye contact with anyone. Instead, she stands very close to me and frowns slightly at Jen.

"You did?" Brad looks horrified. "I overheard them talking about bringing you back for the wedding. I tried to stop them, but they shoved me in a closet."

"Luckily he had his phone." Jen joins in the story. "He

texted me and I let him out. Then we followed the wedding party in a little motorboat." Her eyes cut to Meli. "Did you know Brad can drive a little motorboat in the open ocean?"

"I've got skills." Brad shrugs. "Anyway, when we got to land we asked around if anyone had seen a group of loud and obnoxious men in suits and they pointed us this way. There were a few false starts with folks directing us to guys here on spring break, though, since everyone thought we were talking about swimsuits, not wedding suits."

"We weren't sure what they were going to do," Jen says. "But we had to stop them." Then, she looks back and forth between Meli and me. "Are we interrupting something?"

"No," Meli says. "It's okay. Welcome to Saint Mary. *What* are you wearing?"

"Oh." Jen twirls. "It's my bridesmaid's dress. Isn't it hideous? Sorry, Hannah, did you pick it?"

I shake my head. "I never saw it before."

"Me neither," Meli admits. "I went to the measuring session and put the dress out of my mind. Why are you wearing it, though?"

"Eric told everyone to get ready for photos. I thought it was strange, but I went with it. No one except Hannah's family knew you were gone, and I didn't want to give up the game." Jen waves her hand. "But forget that nonsense. Tell me what happened with Eric and the groomsmen!"

"Hannah kicked Eric in the balls," Meli states matter-of-factly.

"Good job, little sis!" Brad holds up his palm and I slap it. Then I slide my hand back into Meli's. Both Brad and Meli look at our joined hands, and I start to worry. Then I take a deep breath. There's no reason to worry about what they think, because I know what *I* think. Meli is my girlfriend. I won't be ashamed.

"Hannah, is there something you want to tell me?"

I can't tell what Brad is feeling or thinking. *Oh no.* Maybe Brad won't want to be part of my life because of this, and I'll lose him as well as my parents. I want Meli in my life, no matter what, but I'd be sad to lose Brad.

"I…Meli and I…we're together."

"Congrats. This one, I like." Brad smiles at us and I relax into Meli's side. "Meli, be good to my little sister, okay?"

"I will be." Meli pulls me closer.

I've had enough drama for today. Maybe for my whole life. Meli and Jen exchange a look, and Jen gives a tiny thumbs-up I suspect I wasn't supposed to see.

"So, what's good in this town?" Jen looks around. "I don't think I'd be super welcome back on Saint Sofia."

"Do you want different clothes?" Meli suggests.

"Duh." Jen grins to soften the blow of her sarcasm, but I get the feeling that she'd be happy to switch that dress for just about any other outfit.

We all trudge up to the Blue Door and into our small room, where Jen nips into the bathroom to change into one of Meli's dresses. It's both a little too big and somehow much more revealing on her, but she seems happy enough. Brad takes off his suit jacket and tie but is still in his slacks and dress shirt.

"I'm okay like this," he says. "I can find a shop to pick up some board shorts if I get too hot. I have plenty of beach days back home. Lunch?"

We find a little hole-in-the-wall Italian place after just a few minutes of searching. Following the instructions of the seat-yourself sign, we find an empty table in the window. I am a little giddy and I suspect the others feel the same way.

"So, tell me what happened at the wedding after I left." I lean forward, bracing my chin on my hands. Meli raises her eyebrows at me and gives me a little nod. I smile at her. I am fairly comfortable with this group, so it isn't too hard to initiate a conversation.

Jen and Brad exchange glances.

"Well," Jen says, "the night you left, the party kept going until late. Eric was really enjoying himself and...I saw him making out with Crystal. Sorry, Hannah."

"I know. He told me about the two of them. I think they're made for each other."

"They are *totally* made for each other. I'm glad you're out of that situation." Meli holds up her fist and I bump it. Somehow the whole gesture ends with both of our hands on my thigh, mine on top of hers.

"The next day," Brad continues, "we swam with the dolphins, which was pretty sketchy. I think Jen told you."

"Yeah, I'm still looking up how to report it to PETA, like I said I would, but I'm not sure if they're going to do anything about it since they're on a private island." Jen shrugs sadly. "Poor dolphins."

"We also had some nice meals and people did different activities—the island has some trails and a spa and, you know, the pools, and other stuff. Then Eric came to see me and our parents." Brad nods at me. "He told us you ran away and that we needed to help get you back. He assured us it was just nerves that made you take off."

"What did you guys say?" I'm curious to know details, though I have some idea. When Brad looks down sheepishly, I'm even more sure that my parents are finished with me. It's disappointing, but not surprising.

"I said I was sure we should respect any decision you made." Brad grabs his complimentary glass of water and takes a long drink. Maybe he's hoping we'll forget my question. I know my parents were not as gracious nor as respectful as he is. No matter, I want to hear what they said. He continues. "Our parents apologized for you. They said you'd always been a little funny and promised to do their best to get you to come back."

"Charming," Meli mutters.

"That was basically it for the second day. Then the third day was this fiasco." Brad nods, as if satisfied he's told us all the important details. "There are supposed to be post-wedding celebrations for the rest of the week, but that's probably changed. What have you two been up to?"

My face warms at the question. Then Meli starts talking and I realize that, of course, he wasn't talking about all the kissing or the sex last night.

"We had a lot of trouble finding a hotel," she explains. "So, we ended up in the tiny one you visited. Speaking of which, if you guys are staying on Saint Mary tonight, we should really start finding you a room as soon as possible. There's supposed to be one available at our hotel starting tonight. Anyway, the first day we had a nice long walk, ate some good food, and went swimming. Today we bought a turtle, swam some more, and then those jerks found us."

"Tory!" I press my hand to my chest. "I left him on the beach when we ran."

"I'm sorry." Meli squeezes my hand.

"A living turtle?" Jen looks scandalized.

"No, no, an inflatable one," Meli explains quickly.

"Thank goodness. Okay, and obviously you two hooked up."

My cheeks are practically on fire now, but I'm not going to run away from this. I nod, and Meli and I exchange a glance. Happiness rushes into my heart—I've only rarely gotten to exchange glances in my life so far.

"Well, good for you, even if I'd rather not hear details." Brad smiles at us. "Also, I'm starving. What's the food situation?"

As if on cue, a waiter bustles over with a menu. "Can I get any drinks to start?" He has a slight Italian accent, and his nametag reads *Giuseppe*.

"I'll take a mojito," Jen says.

"Beer for me."

"I'll stick with the water, unless you have fresh juice." Meli is speaking my language. There may be nothing better on the island.

"Sure, we have mango, orange, and guava."

"Mango juice, please." All eyes turn to me.

"I…"

"Another mango juice?" Meli suggests. I nod and the waiter bustles off to get our orders as I slump in my seat, completely defeated. Brad starts chuckling. Meli shoots him a look that could freeze lava.

"Sorry, sorry." He waves his hand around a little. "It's just, my little sister can defend herself from a gang of groomsmen, but she can't order a drink in a restaurant."

Okay, that is a little funny. Suddenly, we're all laughing. My laughter may be more out of relief that we've survived what has been the world's strangest destination wedding than actual humor at my inability to order a drink. In the moment, I feel brave, like my difficulty speaking in social situations isn't really that big an obstacle. After all, I can always just kick people. Maybe that's my new thing.

Chapter Nineteen

We order a huge lunch of different kinds of pizza and appetizers. By the time the bruschetta arrives, we've already gotten each other into stitches more than a few times. It's almost enough to make me forget my annoyance at these two for interrupting a special moment.

Although, it might not have been the right time.

It's way too soon to tell Hannah I love her, which I had been on the verge of doing. We were fleeing from rabid groomsmen and Hannah was nearly in tears. Plus, we've only known each other for about a month. We only spent two nights together and had sex twice. Last night. That's probably not enough to count as a real relationship. It wouldn't have been socially acceptable to confess my love then and there.

But as I watch Hannah laughingly poke the edge of a misshapen ball of fried cheese and rice, I remember something else. Hannah doesn't seem to care what's socially acceptable and what isn't. I remember her honestly and vulnerability when she confessed her feelings to me on the beach. Maybe she wouldn't be as scared off as I think.

Even so, we're at lunch with her brother and my best friend. There will be no love confessions in the foreseeable future. The thought is both comforting and somehow sad.

"And then," Jen says, "Meli took a flying leap after the falling cake, and it landed right on her head when she tried to dive under it!"

I snap back to attention while Brad and Hannah laugh.

"What terrible stories are you telling about me now?" I glare at Jen in a mostly joking way.

"Your girlfriend should know about your tendency to panic in baked-good-related situations." Jen is still giggling. "Oh, this other time, I came into the kitchen to find Meli trying to piece together a giant cake out of Oreos and peanut butter, because it was my birthday and she'd burned both of the cakes she'd tried to bake."

Brad laughs, but Hannah looks at me with a grin. "That's actually really sweet. If a little bit of a downer about your baking skills."

"I have other skills," I tell Hannah with a wink. She blushes and I change the subject before more embarrassing stories of me can surface. "Jen once gave a class presentation wearing only her pajamas."

"I forgot that it was my day to present, and I'd slept in!"

"It was a three o'clock class!"

We all laugh at that one.

"Once," Hannah bites her lip, "Brad spent a whole family dinner with two toads in his pockets. At the end of the meal, one of them hopped onto the table and he pretended he hadn't seen it before, even though his other pocket was croaking."

"I forgot about that!" Brad chuckles. "The look on Mom's face when Sir Hops-A-Lot leapt into her mashed potatoes was totally priceless."

"I have a good one," I say, squeezing Hannah's hand. "Once, Hannah kicked an evil groom right between the legs!"

"Yeah!" Hannah beams. "And I'd do it again."

"I don't think he will ever present the opportunity again," Jen says.

We all laugh at that one, too.

"Okay, but this one time, Meli tried to eat—"

"I have the margherita right here," the waiter says, interrupting Jen. It's a good thing, because I'm pretty sure I know the story she was about to tell, and it is not flattering. "And here's the capricciosa."

"Right here in the middle is perfect." Jen gestures to the already-cramped center of the table.

He delicately slides the pizzas between our plates of appetizers and drinks, then sashays away with the air of someone who has just performed an elaborate feat for an unappreciative audience.

We share the pizzas and then a few tiramisus for dessert, all the while chatting and swapping stories. Hannah is much more talkative than I've ever seen her with a group. Maybe she really does feel comfortable around all of us. The thought warms my heart.

"You said your hotel has an empty room, right?" Jen asks once we stumble out onto the street clutching our rounded stomachs.

"It did this morning, at least," Hannah says.

"Uh, do you two mind checking that out on your own?"

"Sure, Meli. Should we meet for dinner?"

"Say around six in front of our hotel?"

"Sure."

We part ways. Brad and Jen head uphill toward the hotel while Hannah and I stay on the street in front of the restaurant.

"What's up?" Hannah grins a little shyly. "It seemed like you wanted them to go away. You want to kiss me again?"

"I won't say no to that." I lean in to press a quick, sweet kiss to her lips. "But I would have done that in front of them, too, if you're okay with it."

"Oh, yes—that's okay. What's up, then?"

I hesitate, then chicken out.

"Want to go for a walk? There's supposed to be a trail to the top of that giant hill."

"Sure." We follow winding cobblestone and pavement roads through the city, which soon melt into narrow dirt tracks ascending through jungle.

"I was thinking about what I'll do when we get back to Portland," Hannah says. We've just finished helping each other up a steep section of trail, and she has a smear of dirt on her cheek.

"Yeah? What are you thinking?"

"I'm going to take about half a year to try taking on some freelance writing clients on the side. And I'll try to volunteer at a bakery and maybe with some kids. Then I'm going to quit my job."

"It sounds like you'll be busy." My heart feels a little heavy. Hannah pursuing her career dreams is obviously a good thing, and I'm genuinely happy for her, but I had hoped we might spend time in the next few months exploring our feelings for each other.

"Yeah." Hannah grins at me, looking very pleased. "But not too busy. I also want to start making friends."

"Okay." I laugh a little at her enthusiasm.

"Yeah." She nods seriously. "I realized that maybe I need to give myself a little more credit. I don't like hanging out with huge groups of dumb people, so I get quiet and nervous, but in small groups of people I like, I do okay."

"You really do. I saw you today at lunch. You seemed relaxed."

Hannah smiles. "I *was*. So, I am actually hoping for your help on that. I wonder if Jen can be my friend. I like her."

"Well, I can't speak for Jen, but I'm sure she'd like to be friends with you."

"Great! Because along with the work stuff and the friends

stuff, there's something else I need to do. And I'll need your help with that, too." For the first time in the conversation, Hannah looks a little shy, and we walk a few steps in relative quiet, the only sound the singing birds in the trees above us and the rustling of the leaves. I know by now that I need to give Hannah space to gather her thoughts, even though I have a strong urge to jump right in to try to help her. Or at least suggest a few potential tasks that I could help her with—mainly of the kissing variety.

"I want to spend time with you," she finally says. She stops, so I stop beside her. She gazes at the trees above us.

"I love you, Meli."

For a moment, I think I've misheard her.

"You love me?"

"Yeah." Now she looks at me. "Is that okay? I was thinking about it, and I know I do. I love spending time with you. I love talking to you. I love having sex with you. You're the most wonderful person I've ever met. But I know it's too soon to say stuff like that. If it's too much, you can just ignore it and we can revisit the idea in a few months."

"I love you, too." I hold out my arms and she steps into a kiss, the kind that speaks of the history we've shared and the future we're building together. My heart might burst with happiness.

"Once again," I say when we finally come up for air, "my wonderful girlfriend proves that she's braver than I am."

"What do you mean?"

"I wanted to tell you that I love you, but I was worried you'd think it was too soon."

"That's me." Hannah nods seriously. "I've proven again and again that I am the perfect judge of how to handle social situations like this."

Laughing, I kiss her again, then we step apart, hands still

clasped, and continue walking. Being with Hannah isn't like being with anyone else. She surprises me all the time, but I also feel very safe with her. She doesn't throw up walls or put on pretenses. She just tells me, with perhaps a little bit of struggle to get the words out, what she wants. I am just lucky that what she wants is me.

The view from the hilltop is gorgeous. There's a viewpoint where the trees have been trimmed to let us look straight down to the island below us and the shining ocean further out. In the distance I see the shadow of an island.

"Is that Saint Sofia?" I point it out.

"Hello, Eric!" Hannah calls out. "I hope you enjoy your bride-less wedding!" We both laugh.

"Can you believe that this all started with me being paid to be your bridesmaid?"

Hannah's eyes widen. "Wait a minute. You aren't…we aren't…because of the payment…"

I can't wait for her to form a clearer sentence. I'm laughing too hard. "You think that we're together because Eric paid me to be a bridesmaid and I took my duties of making you happy on your wedding day too seriously?"

Hannah laughs now, too.

"I guess when you say it like that, it does sound a little ridiculous. Hey, thanks for being my bridesmaid. Even though the wedding isn't happening."

"Any time, love. Although I hope you won't ask me to be your bridesmaid again. It seems like that could get confusing."

Hannah nods seriously. "Don't worry. In any future matrimonial endeavors, I won't accept any bridesmaid other than Crystal."

I make a gagging noise. "I'm so glad that I'm never going to have to see that woman again."

"Same." We lean against each other for a long time, our

arms around each other's waists, and watch the sun glint off the water and the palm trees sway. It's a perfect moment, the kind I wish I could bottle up to open on rainy days. Luckily, I don't have to because this isn't the curtain call. It's just the opening act.

Epilogue

"So, Hannah." Jen holds her fist to my face as though she is brandishing a microphone. "How do you feel on this, your wedding day, take two?"

I glance around the garden. Meli and I have set up fairy lights and a buffet table of tiny cakes. There's a flowery arch at the front of the garden where Brad stands prepared to marry us. Meli's parents are here, laughing with the other guests and sampling the trays of small cakes we have as hors d'oeuvres.

When her father sees me looking, he gives me a friendly wave.

The other guests are Meli's and my friends. There are her colleagues from her performance troupe, kids and parents from the Kew Kids, and her friends from college and high school and childhood. It's a lot of people, so I'm nervous, but I've met them all one by one and I like them, so I'm still able to have a nice time. Then there are my managers at the bakery, Peggy and Sue. They are a pair of slightly older women who have taken me under their wings—and shown me that although baking is incredibly rewarding, it's also a lot harder than I imagined. And there's Carlo, my writing buddy, who I met at a group for writers. We now meet at least once a week to support each other on our various freelance assignments.

And then there's Meli. She wears a white lacy top and a long white skirt. A band of her skin is visible at her waist and her hair is done up around her face with small glass beads. When she looks at me, I see her love and warmth and she waves to me with the tips of her fingers. I wave back.

Jen clears her throat and I turn to her. "I would say that I am feeling amazing. It's a big improvement over wedding day number one."

"Not least of all because of your amazing bridesmaid." Jen gives a little flouncy twirl. She did become my friend. Today, she's a bridesmaid for both me and Meli, dressed in a low-cut, short-skirted purple…dress. She picked it out for herself.

"Of course, mostly thanks to you. Not because I'm marrying someone I love or because I like all the people here or because there are no captive dolphins or raging bigots around."

"Sure, sure, them, too." Jen winks. "But mostly me. Speaking of bigots, do you know how he's doing?"

"I really don't." I shrug. "The last I heard, he married Crystal instead of me on Saint Sofia. I imagine they now spend their time taking candy from babies and shooting stray dogs with miniature bows and arrows."

"I believe it."

"If I could have everyone's attention!" Brad calls from the arch. "Let's get started!"

Jen waves at him and he waves back. The two of them have been dating for almost two years now. Jen eventually moved to California to be with him, but they decided to spend winters in Portland to hang out with us, and we spend a few weeks with them in summer.

Meli waits for me at the beginning of the aisle, and suddenly I have eyes for no one else.

"You look beautiful," she says.

"Thank you. So do you."

"I can't wait to marry you, love."

"I can't wait to marry you, either." Then the music starts, and we link arms to follow a procession of assorted important people in our lives, in no particular order. We decided to walk the aisle together, arm in arm, both because the *father giving daughter away* tradition is a bit outdated and sexist, and because my father refused to be here today. He and my mother never came to terms with me being a lesbian or with me running away from my own wedding. Maybe they'll change their minds one day. Maybe not. Either way, I'm happier now that I'm living my truth, despite a bit of sadness on days like today.

The walk down the aisle takes a small eternity, but soon we're standing at the front of the crowd. My heart starts to race, looking at all those people, and Meli squeezes my hands. It's a gesture of reassurance, repeated hundreds of times since that first time in the café.

"I believe you've prepared your own vows," Brad reminds us. Just as we planned, Meli leans forward and whispers into my ear, her breath warm.

"Hannah, I've liked you since the moment I saw your picture and loved you since the day we ran away from your first wedding. You are truly the bravest, funniest, most interesting person that I know, and I feel lucky every day to call you mine. I promise that I'll love you for as long as we both live."

She pulls away and I lean forward, whispering my own vows into the soft shell of her ear. "Meli, I love you. You've changed my life for the better a million times over, and I hope to do the same for you as we grow and change together. I've never met anyone like you, and I know I never will. You are my one and only."

Whispered vows aren't exactly typical, but nothing about this wedding is. Meli suggested it when I realized I would struggle if I had to stand and recite vows in front of this many people. It's just one of the thousand reasons I love her.

"Rings?" Brad prompts. Meli's dad passes them to us, and

we slip them onto each other's fingers. They are simple silver bands with our names written inside in a beautiful curling script.

"Well, there we go." Brad rocks back on his heels and gestures to us. "You may kiss your bride."

And we do.

About the Author

Haley lives with her partner in Prague, where she spends her time writing, teaching English, and cooking elaborate meals. *Only a Bridesmaid* is her first book.

About the Author

Books Available From Bold Strokes Books

A Heart Divided by Angie Williams. Emmaline is the most beautiful woman Jack has ever seen, but being a veteran of the Confederate army that killed her husband isn't the only thing keeping them apart. (978-1-63679-537-9)

Adrift by Sam Ledel. Two women whose lives are anchored by guilt and obligation find romance amidst the tumultuous Prohibition movement in 1920s California. (978-1-63679-577-5)

Cabin Fever by Tagan Shepard. The longer Morgan and Shelby are stranded together, the more their feelings grow, but is it real, or just cabin fever? (978-1-63679-632-1)

Clean Kill by Anne Laughlin. When someone starts killing people she knows in the recovery world, former detective Nicky Sullivan must race to stop the killer and keep herself from being arrested for the crimes. (978-1-63679-634-5)

Only a Bridesmaid by Haley Donnell. A fake bridesmaid, a socially anxious bride, and an unexpected love—what could go wrong? (978-1-63679-642-0)

Primal Hunt by L.L. Raand. Anya, a young wolf warrior, finds herself paired with Rafe, one of the most powerful Vampires in the Americas, in an erotic union of blood and sex.(978-1-63679-561-4)

Snake Charming by Genevieve McCluer. Playgirl vampire Freddie is on the run and a chance encounter with lamia Phoebe makes them both realize that they may have found the love they'd given up on. (978-1-63679-628-4)

Spirits and Sirens by Kelly and Tana Fireside. When rumored ghost whisperer Elena Murphy and very skeptical assistant fire chief Allison Jones have to work together to solve a 70-year old mystery, sparks fly—will it be enough to melt the ice between them and let love ignite? (978-1-63679-607-9)

Aubrey McFadden Is Never Getting Married by Georgia Beers. Aubrey McFadden is never getting married, but she does have five weddings to attend, and she'll be avoiding Monica Wallace, the woman who ruined her happily ever after, at every single one. (978-1-63679-613-0)

A Case for Discretion by Ashley Moore. Will Gwen, a prominent Atlanta attorney, choose Etta, the law student she's clandestinely dating, or is her political future too important to sacrifice? (978-1-63679-617-8)

The Broken Lines of Us by Shia Woods. Charlie Dawson returns to the city she left behind and meets an unexpected stranger on her first night back, discovering that coming home might not be as hard as she thought. (978-1-63679-585-0)

Flowers for Dead Girls by Abigail Collins. Isla might be just the right kind of girl to bring Astra out of her shell—and maybe more. The only problem? She's dead. (978-1-63679-584-3)

Good Bones by Aurora Rey. Designer and contractor Logan Barrow can give Kathleen Kenney the house of her dreams, but can she convince the cynical romance writer to take a chance on love? (978-1-63679-589-8)

Leather, Lace, and Locs by Anne Shade. Three friends, each on their own path in life, with one obstacle…finding room in their busy lives for a love that will give them their happily ever afters. (978-1-63679-529-4)

Rainbow Overalls by Maggie Fortuna. Arriving in Vermont for her first year of college, an introverted bookworm forms a friendship with an outgoing artist and finds what comes after the classic coming out story: a being out story. (978-1-63679-606-2)

Revisiting Summer Nights by Ashley Bartlett. PJ Addison and Wylie Parsons have been called back to film the most recent *Dangerous Summer Nights* installment. Only this time they're not in love, and it's going to stay that way. (978-1-63679-551-5)

All This Time by Sage Donnell. Erin and Jodi share a complicated past, but a very different present. Will they ever be able to make a future together work? (978-1-63679-622-2)

Crossing Bridges by Chelsey Lynford. When a one-night stand between a snowboard instructor and a business executive becomes more, one has to overcome her past, while the other must let go of her planned future. (978-1-63679-646-8)

Dancing Toward Stardust by Julia Underwood. Age has nothing to do with becoming the person you were meant to be, taking a chance, and finding love. (978-1-63679-588-1)

Evacuation to Love by CA Popovich. As a hurricane rips through Florida, so too are Joanne and Shanna's lives upended. It'll take a force of nature to show them the love it takes to rebuild. (978-1-63679-493-8)

Lean in to Love by Catherine Lane. Will badly behaving celebrities, erotic sex tapes, and steamy scandals prevent Rory and Ellis from leaning in to love? (978-1-63679-582-9)

The Romance Lovers Book Club by MA Binfield and Toni Logan. After their book club reads a romance about an American tourist falling in love with an English princess, Harper and her best friend, Alice, book an impulsive trip to London hoping they'll both fall for the women of their dreams. (978-1-63679-501-0)

Searching for Someday by Renee Roman. For loner Rayne Thomas, her only goal for working out is to build her confidence, but Maggie Flanders has another idea, and neither is prepared for the outcome. (978-1-63679-568-3)

Truly Home by J.J. Hale. Ruth and Olivia discover home is more than a four-letter word. (978-1-63679-579-9)

View from the Top by Morgan Adams. When it comes to love, sometimes the higher you climb, the harder you fall. (978-1-63679-604-8)

Blood Rage by Illeandra Young. A stolen artifact, a family in the dark, an entire city on edge. Can SPEAR agent Danika Karson juggle all three over a weekend with the "in-laws" while an unknown, malevolent entity lies in wait upon her very skin? (978-1-63679-539-3)

Ghost Town by R.E. Ward. Blair Wyndon and Leif Henderson are set to prove ghosts exist when the mystery suddenly turns deadly. Someone or something else is in Masonville, and if they don't find a way to escape, they might never leave. (978-1-63679-523-2)

Good Christian Girls by Elizabeth Bradshaw. In this heartfelt coming of age lesbian romance, Lacey and Jo help each other untangle who they are from who everyone says they're supposed to be. (978-1-63679-555-3)

Guide Us Home by CF Frizzell and Jesse J. Thoma. When acquisition of an abandoned lighthouse pits ambitious competitors Nancy and Sam against each other, it takes a WWII tale of two brave women to make them see the light. (978-1-63679-533-1)

Lost Harbor by Kimberly Cooper Griffin. For Alice and Bridget's love to survive, they must find a way to reconcile the most important passions in their lives—devotion to the church and each other. (978-1-63679-463-1)

Never a Bridesmaid by Spencer Greene. As her sister's wedding gets closer, Jessica finds that her hatred for the maid of honor is a bit more complicated than she thought. Could it be something more than hatred? (978-1-63679-559-1)

The Rewind by Nicole Stiling. For police detective Cami Lyons and crime reporter Alicia Flynn, some choices break hearts. Others leave a body count. (978-1-63679-572-0)

Turning Point by Cathy Dunnell. When Asha and her former high school bully Jody struggle to deny their growing attraction, can they move forward without going back? (978-1-63679-549-2)

When Tomorrow Comes by D. Jackson Leigh. Teague Maxwell, convinced she will die before she turns 41, hires animal rescue owner Baye Cobb to rehome her extensive menagerie. (978-1-63679-557-7)

You Had Me at Merlot by Melissa Brayden. Leighton and Jamie have all the ingredients to turn their attraction into love, but it's a recipe for disaster.(978-1-63679-543-0)